PAYBACK IS HELL

BOOK III OF THE EVIL STRYKER SERIES

WES RAND

ISBN: 978-1-4834-8103-6 (sc)
ISBN: 978-1-4834-8102-9 (e)

Lulu Publishing Services rev. date: 02/06/2018

PROLOGUE

olonel Nelson Miles had at last received orders to pursue the Sioux, Lakota, and Cheyenne, warriors of Crazy Horse and Two Moons, and defeat them, thereby exacting revenge for the killing of his good friend George Armstrong Custer. The Tongue River Valley in the Montana Territory had nearly three feet of snow in some places with temperatures at minus 30 degrees that January 1877.

Captain Neville Stryker, field artillery officer under Colonel Miles, had been ill with dysentery. Treated with pine leaves mixed in egg whites, his symptoms had subsided, however the illness left him weak from constant bouts of diarrhea and vomiting. Nevertheless, Stryker convinced Colonel Miles to send him and an Apsaalooke scout called Many Coups, along with five men from E' Troop, Sergeant Cory, Corporal Sager, and Privates Richards, Johnson, and Bales, to search for two missing scouts. The scouts had been making daily reconnoitering patrols looking for the whereabouts of Chief Sitting Bull. They had not returned from the day before.

A foot of fresh snow made travel arduous. The men wore buffalo robes over their many layers of army issue clothing making them look like winter trappers rather than soldiers. They started out before daybreak. The morning was cold and the snow crackled under their horses hooves. However, the sky cleared and, when the sun finally came up, it warmed the air, somewhat.

Stryker and his men found the two scouts after three hours of tramping through the heavy snow. Overlooking an encampment that Many Coups said was Northern Cheyenne, Stryker looked through his binoculars and spied the two men trussed up between animal hide skinning poles. Spread-eagled and naked, they hung back to back, their wrists and ankles lashed to vertical posts. Stryker impassively watched one the Cheyenne squaws efficiently filet strips two-inches wide from the collarbone to the groin. As she dug the blade into the skin to begin each strip, he could see the soldier flinch, barely, but enough to show he was alive.

Captain Stryker lowered the glasses. "The two are down there. Nothing can be done for them."

"Are they alive?" Sergeant Cory asked, bringing up his horse.

A wave of nausea struck Stryker. He bent over, retching. "Not for long."

"Sir, can I have a look sir?" Cory extended his hand.

Stryker handed the binoculars to Sergeant Cory and said, "We're heading back."

"Like hell I am," the sergeant growled, still peering through the glasses. "They're still alive. We can't leave 'em like that." He passed the binoculars to Corporal Sager. "Ain't no braves down there! Just them fuckin' squaws. I'm . . . gonna . . . kill . . . 'em." Cory drove the words through grinding teeth.

"Our orders are to find them and the Sioux. I figure those Cheyenne are heading for Sitting Bull. If they see us, we've lost the element of surprise. Mount up!" Stryker barked.

"I'm going down there! Who's going with me?" Sergeant Cory looked hard at Corporal Sager, then the other troopers, one at a time. "Them squaws are skinin' 'em alive. Got 'em hangin' from poles, skinin' 'em like they was . . . like animals!"

"I'm wit ya!" Corporal Sager said, still staring through the binoculars. He brought them down to his chest then tossed them aside. He pulled the rifle from its scabbard and led his horse next to Sergeant Cory's.

Privates Richards and Johnson, already saddled up, heeled their mounts to bring them behind Sager's. Private Bales, who had been standing by Sergeant Cory, stomped angrily toward his horse. "I'm going too, sir."

Stryker leapt behind Bales, pulling a straight razor from under the buffalo robe. He threw his arm around the Private's neck, locked a forearm under the chin, and lifted hard. He threw the blade against Bales' naked throat and dragged him around to face the Sergeant.

"We're going back."

Sergeant Cory's jaw slacked open. "Good God, Captain. You've gone mad!" Even if he had wanted to challenge Stryker, his heavy coat prevented easy access to a gun.

Stryker dug the razor in, drawing blood. "Mount up."

Corporal Sager rebooted his rifle. "Them two men are hangin' naked in this cold, Sarge. An' I reckon the Captain's right. They ain't gonna make it."

Whether or not Corporal Sager actually believed what he said is not known. But, the men knew Stryker would kill Bales. They had seen the Captain kill. They had seen him take a life without expression and not in the heat of battle or in anger. He dealt death mechanically, efficiently. He would end Bales' life the same way.

"I'll have to report this sir." Sergeant Cory remained in place a few moments, waiting for the threat to sink in.

"Private Bales will remain with me and Many Coups." Stryker motioned with his head for the Sergeant to leave.

The Sergeant saluted and retreated to his horse. Once mounted, he ordered, "Let's go."

Stryker waited for the troops to get out of sight before he released the young Private. Bales stepped away, rubbing his neck. Stryker walked past him, grabbed the binoculars' strap, and pulled the half buried glasses out of the snow.

Bales suddenly looked around, searching. "Sir, where's Many Coups?"

"Many Coups here." The Crow rounded a wooded knoll dragging a woman behind him. A squaw dressed in multi-layered animal hides, clumsily clawing at the hand buried in her hair, struggled against his strong grip. She abandoned his hand and grabbed at a sapling, willing to have her hair ripped out rather than be captured. Many Coups gave a vicious jerk and she lost her hold. The woman uttered not a sound but she fought with all her might.

"Squaw hid. Look for firewood. She Cheyenne."

"Ask her about Sitting Bull, Crazy Horse." Stryker ordered. He turned away, coughing, struggling to repress the urge to vomit.

Many Coups used hand signs as he spoke Cheyenne. He pulled the blanket from around her neck. Her long black mane fell disheveled to her shoulders and Many Coups brushed back the hair with his hand. Her beauty was striking. High cheekbones, straight nose, unlike the round flat ones of her race, and sparkling blue eyes, produced a beautiful portrait of the mixed blood in her veins. "She say she not know. She not talk. No tell name."

"Ask again." Stryker spit bile onto the snow.

Many Coups slapped the woman hard with back of his hand, then gripping her by the shoulders he repeated the questions. He hurled them at her with jagged edges. She shook her head. He looked at Stryker, waited.

"Rides with you, Bales."

"E-e-e-e-i-i-i-i." The Cheyenne warrior suddenly emerged from the trees and lunged at Many Coups, spear leveled at the Crow's mid-section. Many Coups turned at the instant the lance pierced his abdomen, driving the six-inch flint tip into his liver. The warrior wrenched the spear from Many Coups stomach and launched himself at Stryker.

Stryker deflected the shaft, blocking it with the sai fixed upside down on his forearm. He made a small circular movement with the sai hand and leveled his arm. The Cheyenne's momentum carried him forward and Stryker's elbow slammed into the warrior's temple. Stryker clutched a clump of thick black hair in his left hand and jerked downward. The warrior doubled at the waist and fell forward. Dropping to one knee, Stryker drove the center prong through the back of the Cheyenne's neck.

Stryker walked over to Many Coups, who struggled to sit.

The Crow's blood seeped onto the snow, turning it black. He looked up at Stryker. "You give Many Coups joy. I watch he who kill me, die."

"Sir, there wuz another injun. He ran off when he saw you kill that one." The girl had been kneeling next to the Cheyenne and Private Bales jerked her to her feet.

Stepping behind the dying Crow, Stryker drew his revolver and fired a bullet into Many Coups' head.

"Private Bales, secure his gun and put her on your horse." Stryker kicked the Cheyenne over. His lifeless eyes stared skyward. Stryker mounted and waited for Bales to settle in the saddle ahead of the young squaw.

They had ridden two miles when the gun shot caused Stryker to wheel about. He had pulled the rifle half out of the scabbard before he saw the girl roll off the horse's back.

"I had the gun slung over my shoulder. She pulled it out. I didn't feel nothing." Private Bales jumped to the ground, knelt beside the prostrate girl, and saw the blood welling up through the hole in her chest. "She's dead. She killed herself. What she do that for?" He looked at Stryker

"Pick up the gun. Let's go." Stryker goaded his horse frontward.

~~~~~~~~~~~~

"Sir, you're to report to Colonel Miles." The Corporal ran up to Stryker and saluted just as the Captain's boots hit the ground. He returned the salute and started off on the frozen footpath toward the Headquarters tent.

"Captain, I got the report from Sergeant Cory. Do you have anything to add?" Colonel Miles glanced up from the map board on his desk.

"A Cheyenne warrior attacked and killed our scout, Many Coups. I managed to kill the warrior but another Cheyenne saw us and escaped. We captured a squaw. She killed herself about three miles west of us. Sergeant Cory is a good soldier. I won't add anything to his account."

"The Cheyenne attack occurred after Cory left your position?" Stryker nodded.

"Well, the Indians know we have scouts in the area. They may not know our strength." The Colonel paused. "Captain, I'm sending you back to the Department of the Missouri Command, General

Sheridan. You'll leave immediately. But before you go, report back here. I'll have sealed orders to take with you. That's all."

Captain Stryker did not know until he met with General Sheridan, the sealed documents contained a recommendation for his promotion to Major.

CHAPTER ONE

several years passed and now Stryker was on a train rolling from the logging town of Felton, California.

Smoke from the Shay locomotive stole its way into the coach car. At a curve in the tracks a sudden breeze flooded into the car's open windows, filling the interior with a cloud of vapors and ashes. The female passengers squealed and coughed, covering their faces with handkerchiefs, and gruff, vulgar curses from the men greeted the unwelcome smoke. Even the soldiers in blue uniforms, who made up two-thirds of the riders, began coughing into their hands.

"Open the rear door!" The man in a brown tweed suit ordered. He rose to his feet and banged open the forward door.

A trooper seated on a back bench who wore no stripes on his sleeves, sprang to follow the order. He and the other soldiers sat on the bench seats as if in formation. At the front an infantry officer, Captain Talbot, sat next to Neville Stryker dressed in a black shirt and denim pants. A drooping mustache and a ten-day old beard with strands of gray matched the color of the long, straight hair brushing his shoulders. The worn and dusty low-rimed black Stetson hat rested atop a lean six-foot, three-inch frame when he unfolded to his full height. Rough around the edges, he is not a nice man, but he has few enemies. That's because most of them were left dead after confronting him. Wiser ones stayed away and kept their mouths shut. He made no friends. When he gazed at someone, his predatory eyes warned that he lived on a razor's edge of violence. If people knew his bloody past, they might think his favorite color was red. He came into people's lives and moved on. Although thankful he left, they couldn't forget him. Hardly a ladies man, the fierceness of his features put most women off. Few considered him handsome. Years of hard-riding and harsh weather had worn off stamped letters of his name from the saddle skirt. Most people said what now showed best fit the man— EVIL STRYKER.

Two sergeants were seated behind the Captain and Stryker, with corporals and privates in descending rank toward the rear.

Occasionally, Talbot would speak to the man next to him, whose replies were short, not curt, but short, with no invitation for more talk. Eventually, the officer pulled his cap down over his brow and left the other man to his own thoughts.

The unfriendly man, Stryker, had other things on his mind, notably the letter Talbot handed him after being rescued from a mob of loggers aiming to kill him.

Stryker sat, straight-backed, staring out the window, idly watching the wooded landscape passing by. He kept his rigid posture not due to military habit, his time in uniform having ended more than fifteen years earlier. Rather he had crawled so far back into the caverns of his mind, he simply forgot to relax. The piercing gray eyes, set recessed between sharp ledges for brows and high cheekbones that accentuated the hollowness beneath them, watched scenes passing by the window but the images failed to register. Now a letter, and the woman who wrote it, crowded back into his life. His plans had been to live alone, carrying the tragic memories of his long dead wife as his only companion. Now, just a few months ago, this woman had boldly changed things for him. The corners of his mouth twitched when he thought about their first time together. He'd thought her dead too, killed like so many before. Recently, he learned she lived. And now he carried the letter she'd written in his coat pocket. It showed final proof she was still of this world.

Dear Neville,
Lucas said how you broke his nose when he told you I died from the gunshot that night. He deserved it. He even said so himself.

2

I never expected to see you again; that our time had passed. Then, there you were on the pier. You saw me too. I could tell. It now seems as if our paths may cross again.

I work for George Hearst, a very wealthy Senator, and a miner like myself. He needs help collecting on a wager he'd fairly made and won. It is a delicate matter. I told him how persuasive you could be.

When I learned soldiers were being sent to Felton and that you might be there, I asked Mr. Hearst to have this letter delivered to you.

Thank you,

Morgan Bickford

Neville, it would be a lie to say I don't think of you often.

What did she mean by "persuasive?" He wondered. Certainly not by his talking–too few words for that. With a gun? Or, maybe it was the way he took her when they first met? Would she know he'd figure both? Probably, Morgan could be persuasive too. She moved well enough under him.

And that last line. It took a lot for her to write it. Got to think. Got to think real hard, he thought.

"Major Stryker?"

Stryker snapped his head up to see the Sergeant standing in the aisle with yellow chevrons cascading down his sleeves.

Captain Talbot pushed back his cap, glancing first at the Sergeant, and then with arched eyebrows, he turned to Stryker.

"I told 'em you was him. You ain't in uniform but there ain't no mistakin' your eyes sir," the Sergeant bragged, as if he'd won a bet.

"Sergeant Bales," Stryker replied.

"Yes sir. I told 'em," nodding at the soldiers behind the Captain and Stryker, "how you almost cut my throat. An' you'd been right to done it too. Them injuns woulda' killed us all and the rest back in camp, if they knowed we wuz around. We sure made 'em pay after you shipped out though. Them two squaws that did the skinnin'. . . " Sergeant Bales shifted his attention to Captain Talbot, and then looked around to find everyone, including the women, was listening.

"You still carry that big fork thing?" Bales asked.

The weapon the sergeant referred to was a sai, a Chinese farming tool later used as a defense weapon against the sword. Stryker's Chinese uncle taught him how to fight with it as a boy growing up in San Francisco. A sinister looking weapon, it had three prongs with the center prong being the longest. Stryker had filed all three to needle point sharpness and more than a few men had taken their last breaths watching their own blood flow down its tines.

Stryker ignored the question.

Bales returned to their last encounter. "They all paid sir, including them damn squaws. Good to see you again sir. Heard you got promoted." He started to salute but stopped his hand inches from his brow as if realizing Stryker was out of uniform. Stryker dipped his head slightly and Bales resumed the salutation with a snappy finish. "Told you all," he said, as he returned to his seat.

CHAPTER TWO

"**A**re you still in the army?" Captain Talbot asked Stryker, interrupting the recollections Bales had referenced.

"No."

The train continued north after stopping in San Jose. Neither man spoke until the train pulled into San Francisco's Ferry House at the end of Market Street. Captain Talbot gave instructions for the care and stabling of Stryker's horse and the two of them caught the Market Street Cable Car Railway to the Palace Hotel.

Stryker watched as the cable car moved toward them. It stopped at the Ferry House and rotated on a large wooden disc. People got off and others clamored on as it turned, seemingly impervious to the mechanics and marvel of it all.

"Let's hop on," Captain Talbot said, stepping onto the rotating platform and climbing on the cable car. Perhaps he purposely left off "sir" as small retribution for Stryker's rudeness on the train. After all, the man said he wasn't in the army anyway.

Stryker followed without comment.

A grip man stood up front working waist high levers, releasing and locking a clamping device connected to an underground cable. The car, crowded with passengers, lurched forward and started up Market Street, traveling about four miles an hour, steadily passing horse-drawn buggies and wagons weaving back and forth across the rails, some missing the front bumper by inches. The wagon drivers on their way to various unknown destinations traversed Market Street from side to side for no apparent reason. Men dressed in suits and women in bustled dresses carrying parasols, crossed nonchalantly in front of the slow moving car.

Stryker looked about the cable car and realized that he, in trail-riding clothing and wearing a gun belt slung low, seemed out of place. He returned stares with menacing looks, causing those who gawked to turn their eyes.

More than twenty years had passed since Stryker's uncle sent him east, intending to provide his young nephew with an education from the nation's best schools and universities. His mother, a mixed breed, mostly Asian, and his Norwegian father, had been stabbed to death by dock worker thugs protecting their jobs on the wharf. His mother's brother was determined to keep the promise he'd made to her—proper schooling. But Stryker got caught up in the Civil War when he was fifteen and afterward was appointed to West Point by his commanding general. He got the education, even gained a promising position with the House of Morgan upon leaving the army years later.

He married Leigh, and lost her in a tragic accident. He'd murdered the man most responsible. And then after that it seemed as if someone was always pissing in an open cut.

The one and two story wooden buildings he remembered along Market Street had been torn down and replaced with brick and block structures, some of them towering seven floors to the sky. The town had moved on without him.

"We get off here," Captain Talbot said, rising to his feet. He grabbed a brass pole and slung his body from the moving cable car to the street. Much to the relief of the other passengers, Stryker did the same.

The Captain led Stryker up to a seven story building with the name Palace Hotel stamped proudly over a large arched entryway. They walked through a smaller door beside the entryway and, once inside, Stryker realized the larger door was for carriages. Two of them, all shiny and black, were parked along the circular curb of the marbled promenade, a roundabout for horse and buggy. The outside of the hotel did not belie the spectacle of the Palace within its walls. Brightly painted white columned tiers of verandas stretched to the sky-lighted ceiling above. Large potted plants, some as large as twelve feet high, were scattered about a tropical garden adorned with statuaries and fountains.

After taking a few steps along the roundabout perimeter, they paused to take in the hotel's grandeur. "Something, ain't it," Talbot said. "Seven hundred and fifty-five rooms, each one with its own bath. It's the world's finest hotel. The locals call it the Bonanza Inn."

"Where's Hearst?"

"Senator Hearst," the Captain told Stryker, seizing upon the opportunity to rebuke him. But he wondered if he had overstepped his bounds, seeing how the Senator had sent him to escort this man. Talbot drew his head back and admired the top floors, illuminated by the sun's rays streaking through the sky-lights. "He's a United States Senator, sir. He's probably in . . . hey! Where you going?"

But, Stryker had already passed under one of several columned archways on his way to the men's reception area, referred to as The Office Room. He walked into a cavernous room with an inlaid marble floor and even more arches rose upward twenty feet to a ceiling. The floor led to a large ornately carved rosewood reception desk. An attaché, wearing a blazer with an embroidered insignia of the Palace Hotel on the breast pocket, pushed his way through the male guests, all wearing suits and hats. He clicked his heels, gave a short, curt bow, and then extended his white-gloved hand in a welcoming greeting.

"Looking for a man named Hearst. Supposed to be a Senator," Stryker said, ignoring the offered hand.

The staff member glanced at the holstered .44. He struggled to maintain diplomacy as he said, "I don't know if he's in the hotel sir. Who shall I say is . . .?"

"Major Stryker and Captain Talbot," the Captain said, approaching on Stryker's left. "He's expecting us."

When he saw the uniformed officer, a look of relief spread across the young man's face. "Just a moment, please. I think he's on premises. I'll find him for you. Be right back. Would you care to wait in the Men's Grill Room?

Captain Talbot placed a hand on Stryker's back and pointed his other hand with an open palm. "Shall we have a drink and perhaps something to eat while we wait? He's a busy man. It may be a while."

White linen table cloths, dark mahogany chairs with padded leather seats, a marble and mahogany bar, and mirrored walls were all softly illuminated with hanging gas lamps. The grill was crowded, some men at the bar, others occupying most of the tables. Cigar smoke in long drifts hung below the ceiling. Excited voices flooded the room as occupants in separate gatherings discussed business deals. Occasionally, some of those gathered would erupt in boisterous, hardy laughter.

A waiter in a white dinner jacket greeted the two men. "Welcome to the Men's Grill, a table for two?" He stepped backward. Both men smelled fresh off the trail.

"Yes," the Captain said.

Upon directing them to a table for private conversations, the waiter asked, "Would the gentlemen like to check their weapons?"

Stryker drilled him with an icy glare.

Captain Talbot intervened. "There'll be no trouble from us unless you insist on taking them." He eyed Stryker as if to imply an accord had been reached and let's leave it at that.

They'd barely finished their steak and eggs, washed down with two cups of coffee each when the attaché approached their table. "Senator Hearst will see you now, sir," he said to Stryker. Then he faced Talbot. "And he asked me to express his sincere appreciation to you sir. He also said to tell you that a letter of commendation will be forwarded to your commanding officer." He withdrew a pencil and an envelope from his breast pocket. "May I have the name of your Regimental Commander, sir? He asked that I get it, sir."

At this Captain Talbot straightened smartly but did not rise from his chair. "Colonel Graham, sir, Colonel Graham of the Presidio, Regimental Commander there."

Having heard enough "sirs", Stryker got to his feet. "Where is he?" He figured it was obvious that Hearst wanted him to come alone and it was time to meet the Senator.

Stryker and the attaché took a "rising room" to the seventh floor and the staff member knocked on the double door entrance to suite *702*. A middle-aged man who turned out not to be the Senator, but his personal aid, opened the door. Senator George Hearst sat at the far window of a large spacious sitting room, sparsely appointed with dark wooded mahogany furniture. Overstuffed chairs sat around a conference table. Two leather wingback chairs sat next to a round table with a reading lamp. Wallpaper drawn with dark green figures on white background decorated the walls and Persian rugs covered much of the polished mahogany floor. Hearst turned from looking out at the city and the bay to greet Stryker.

The Senator's aid and the hotel attaché left the room, quietly drawing the doors closed behind them.

"Morgan didn't tell me you were a Major," Hearst said as he came forward, extending a rough and cracked hand. He looked to be in his late sixties, rail thin, and with a full graying beard. His eyes shone sharp, intelligent, and steady, but not intense like Stryker's. He gripped Stryker's hand as he might a pick handle, hard and firm.

"She said you had a job."

Many called Stryker a ruthless, cold-blooded killer; and a man whose fierce eyes warned he had no soul. But, he did have his own code. This man Hearst had sent troops to Felton, thereby saving his life. And now, he had a debt to repay.

"You have children?" The Senator asked, as he guided Stryker to the leather chairs by the reading table.

"No."

"I have a son. He's in his twenties now and hasn't done shit with his life." Hearst spoke with a slight tinge of resignation, maybe even disappointment. "His mother dragged him all over Europe, to museums, plays, and such. Filled his head with *culture*." He hit the "c" hard and made no secret of his dislike for the arts.

"You need a babysitter. Not me." Stryker started to rise.

The Senator raised his hand. "Hold on. A few years ago I won a newspaper in a poker game, *The Examiner*. It's run at a loss since then. And now, William wants to take it over. That's my boy's name, William Randolph." He hesitated a moment. "But there's a problem."

Stryker sat back down.

"The bastard who lost the paper never officially signed it over to me. I let him run it since I don't know shit about newspapers and I felt bad about taking it from him in the first place. Not now though. All this time I thought I owned the thing but Alain, that's his name, Alain Montel, tricked me. Gave me a fake deed-- I don't read too good, Stryker. When I tried to legally give the newspaper to William, I learned the deed was fake."

Hearst reached for an envelope on the table and handed it to Stryker. "He needs to sign this. Probably been stealing from me too . . . why I ain't made no money with it."

Stryker opened the envelope and unfolded the four pages within. After reading them, triggering Hearst's acknowledgement of his literacy with a nod and a grunt, he re-folded the papers and inserted them back into the envelope. "Where do I find him?"

"You don't want to know what I'll pay you?"

Stryker rose from his chair. "Up to you."

Hearst began to stand as well, but with considerable effort, and he settled back in the leather chair. "As you can see dammit, I don't get around too good." He cleared his throat with a deep rattling, cough. "I most likely don't have a lot of time left." With an obvious display of grit, he struggled to his feet and extended his rough and calloused hand. When Stryker took it, he held on while he spoke. "You bring them letters back signed 'fore I die and I'll give you a hundred-thousand dollars."

Stryker and Hearst held each other's gaze momentarily, long enough for a mutual understanding.

As Stryker turned to leave, Hearst called after him. "I secured a room for you while you're in San Francisco. Ask for it at the registration desk. And, as for Montel, I don't know where he is. I sent a man to find him and he ain't come back. That was two months ago. Maybe start with the newspaper office."

Stryker gave a short nod and left, closing the door behind him. The sum promised him would set him up for life. He realized the importance of the son's future to Hearst but he wondered if there was another reason for such a huge amount of money. Morgan? He remembered he didn't get forty percent of her ranch and mine if she'd managed to sell it. She would still owe him that.

Stryker picked up the room key and placed fourteen-hundred dollars in a hotel lock box. He left the Palace and walked up Montgomery Street as a light drizzle began to fall. Although still afternoon, the sun couldn't penetrate the cloud bank hugging the city, and it had grown dark. Businesses started closing for the day. Employees spilled out from multi-storied brick buildings onto the sidewalks, joining others already walking home. One of the hotel attachés had given Stryker directions to the newspaper office. Water dripped steadily off his Stetson before he came to the small single-story building housing *The Examiner*. It sat on a large lot between Sacramento and Leidesdorf Streets. It had been a long damn day, and now dripping wet as he was, he regretted not waiting to look for Montel in the morning.

He tried the doorknob and found it locked. He rapped on the door.

"We're closed!" A man's gravelly voice responded.

Stryker knocked again, harder.

"I told you dammit, we're closed!" A man a half-head shorter than Stryker, slight of build and wearing an inked-stained apron and spectacles perched on the crown of his bald head, threw open the door. He then tried to slam it shut.

Stryker 's foot blocked it. He shoved the man back and kicked the door closed. "You Montel?"

"No!"

"Where is he?"

"Uh, he . . ."

"You have a lot riding on this . . ." Stryker quickly surveyed the print office and then fixed his steely gaze on the typesetter who started to back away.

"Winslow, I'm Winslow. Mister Montel's not here. He left."

"Sit down." Stryker propped a leg over the corner of a desk. "When will he be back?"

"I never know," the man said, nervously shaking his head side to side. "He comes in, drops off what he wants in the paper and leaves. Please mister, I've got a wife and three . . ."

"Don't want to hear about your bad luck," Stryker growled, dropping his hand to the butt of the Peacemaker.

"Ah Toy's! Maybe Layla!" The typesetter stared at the hand draped over the Colt. "On Sacramento Street, in Chinatown." He looked up at Stryker. "Ah Toy's is a brothel. Layla works there. He's talked about her. Told me several times I needed . . ."

"What's Montel look like?"

Remembering Stryker didn't know Montel, seemed to ease Winslow's anxiety. "Slight of build, dark skin, black hair, he's French. Might be there now," he added, hoping the fiercesome looking man would leave.

"Like I said, Winslow, you've got a lot riding on this." Stryker lowered his leg to the floor and turned for the door. He opened it, and stopped, and drew halfway around. He said, "There's a lot of politics in the paper. That your doing?"

"No sir. Mister Montel's." Then the typesetter added, "But, I set the type. I mean, he . . . uh . . . I . . ." The door slammed shut and he exhaled. "Thank you, God."

Stryker walked up Montgomery to Sacramento Street. The distinctive smells of Chinatown, opium raw and cooked; cigar smoke; tobacco leaves dry and wet, fried, grilled, and raw fish; boiled and steamed vegetables of every kind, wafted in his direction two blocks away—all familiar and repugnant. He found Ah Toy's at Pike Street in the white prostitution section next to the Chinese Mission Church. He figured most visitors probably went to Ah Toy's prior to asking forgiveness next door.

The whore house was a three story building, bricked at ground level. Rotted, bare and wooden slats covered floors two and three. Three girls leaned over the second floor balcony looking for business. Other than them, the bordello offered no outside indication of a rather unremarkable-looking house of pleasure. Stryker climbed two steps and opened the door.

A tall, slender, attractive Asian woman approached him wearing a red Cheongsam dress with a high neck collar and slit sides. Although past her prime, she had kept much of her allure. A dab of rouge accentuated her high cheekbones below eyes which Stryker thought looked both friendly and cruel.

"Welcome to Ah Toy." She smiled, dipping her head of perfectly spun hair. "You first time?"

"Looking for Alain Montel."

"Disc'etion is numba one 'ule, Mista . . . ?"

Figuring Ah Toy's had a good relationship with the local police, Stryker elected not to threaten force, or use it. "Stryker. Layla here?"

"She is!" Ah Toy replied quickly. "But Mista St'yka, you must leave you gun downstai's."

Stryker pulled the Peacemaker and laid it across on her outstretched palms. "Your name Miss?"

"Ah Toy."

"Where's Layla?"

"Third floo, end of the hall." Ah Toy touched his arm as he started to turn. "Two dolla's. Mista St'yka, two dolla's fi'st." She bowed again.

Kerosene lamps with wicks rolled low provided scant light in the hallway and stairs. Two doors closed above him then he passed two men coming down. Although he brushed closely by each man, he couldn't clearly see their faces. Dimness for Ah Toy's rules of discretion, he figured. His boots, and those of the other two men, thumped on wooden steps, interrupting an eerie silence in the hall. Conversations, and presumed sexual activities in rooms, seemed trapped behind the closed doors.

Stryker climbed two flights and made his way down the hall. He stopped at the last door and knocked.

"Come in-n." The woman's voice, barely perceptible from the other side of the door, sounded light and inviting . . . and friendly, at odds with the dark, wood-planked hallway.

He turned the knob, pushed the door open, and stepped inside.

Red velvet wallpaper lined the interior. A maroon flowered rug covered the floor. To his right a pink Victorian lamp, with hanging white tassels, sat on a small round table in a corner. Next to it lay the brass bed and the chaise lounge.

Stryker took in the room but barely noticed the walls or the furniture, because of a stunning, raven-haired beauty with lips the color of blood. She lay on the chaise with her black bodice unlaced and pulled open. She looked up at him, then cupped a snow white breast in her hand and ran her tongue around a cherry red nipple.

It only took a half-second for Stryker to recognize she was a diversion. But that was too long. The blackjack whacked him just above his left ear.

Stryker's eyes fluttered open some time later.

"I wondered how long you'd sleep, mister man," Layla said. Stryker's eyes narrowed to a painful squint. "She sat beside him on the bed and used her forefinger to tap out each word on his bare chest. "You've––been––out––almost––an––hour."

Stryker attempted to sit up, and then he realized his wrists and ankles were bound to the four brass posts. He managed to raise his head, and strained to gaze down his body. Naked, it'd felt like it. Damn. He dropped back on the mattress and rolled his head sideways. Whoever hit him had left.

"He had to leave," she said. The corners of her lips turned up to show a wry smile .

"Montel."

"Uh, huh."

"Took all your money too––'cept for ten dollars he gave me. Said that was to entertain you for a while."

"While he escapes."

"Uh, huh. What you want him for?"

Stryker swung his head around awkwardly and then back to Layla. "My clothes."

"Downstairs, along with everything else." She stretched an arm to the lamp table and grabbed the sai. "What you doing with this, mister?"

"Cover me up damnit!"

Layla put two fingers on his chest and walked them down his abdomen. Twirling a forefinger in pubic hair, she said, "Not yet."

Stryker rested his head back on the bed. "Shit."

"You paid ten dollars, and how much downstairs––two? Yeah, two, I bet."

"This's not my style lady," Stryker growled through gritted teeth.

Layla ran a long, black-painted fingernail around his testicles, and then up the underside of his penis. "I'm supposed to entertain you. Alain's a real gentleman, don't you think?"

Stryker felt an involuntary response.

"Oooh, look at you!" She wrapped her fingers around his erect penis and began stroking. "But wait." She pulled her hand away and stood up. Lifting her dress, she straddled him, and settled herself down on his rigid shaft. She opened the bodice again, revealing the white breasts with their red nipples. She leaned forward and picked up the sai. Pricking the skin, she drew the tip down his chest and blood beaded up in a six-inch line. She left the sai on his chest and straightened.

"Now, just lay there and bleed for me, cowboy."

He had to watch.

Layla closed her eyes and tilted back her head. She cupped both breasts and squeezed their nipples with thumbs and forefingers as she began to rock her hips back and forth. Intermittent moans, low ones he could barely hear, welled up from deep within her throat. After several minutes, she fell forward and jammed the heels of her palms against his shoulders. Her nails dug in his back. Her face was just inches away. She opened her eyes, locked them on his, and let the tips of her long black hair dance on his chest. Her mouth parted. A groan rose up from her navel and escaped her red lips. A warm, gentle breath broke through the sweet fragrance of her perfume and bathed his face.

Stryker lay back and relaxed all but one significant body part. "Well . . . all right. Work it Layla."

And she did.

Layla entertained Stryker two more times before daybreak.

15

CHAPTER THREE

"**H**ere's your clothes," Layla said, closing the door. "You can get your gun downstairs." She laid the garments on the bed next to Stryker sitting with a towel around his waist. "If I knew where he was, I might tell you. I'd tell Alain you drove a hard bargain." Layla stood with hands on her hips, displaying a faint hint of a smile.

"Besides here and the newspaper, where does he go?" Stryker asked, shoving his feet through the trouser legs. He felt the straight razor in his rear pocket.

"If I knew what you wanted with him, I might try to find out."

"I'm not out to kill him."

Stryker finished getting dressed and, downstairs Ah Toy handed him his gun.

"Please visit 'Ah Toy's' again," Ah Toy had said, bowing as she'd presented the .44.

Early risers filtered onto the streets and sidewalks, passing Stryker on his way back to the Palace Hotel. The sky had cleared and the morning sun cast streams of sunlight between the buildings. The warmth from the sun felt good. His shoulders ached and his wrists and ankles were sore from being lashed to the bed posts. He hadn't slept all night. He needed rest.

Hearst had rented a room for him on the third floor, facing north, with a view from Montgomery Street to the bay. The scenery didn't matter to Stryker who slept past noon. Then his brain, trained by years of light sleeping, alerted him that someone had scraped a sealed envelope under the door. It was addressed to him and penned in small neat letters. He opened it and unfolded the page contained within.

"You were followed to your hotel. They know Senator Hearst paid for your room. A. T."

Why, he wondered, would Ah Toy risk sending him the warning?

Winslow turned off the print press to reset type for the next page. He turned and looked up in time for the heel of Stryker's palm to flatten the cartilage in his nose. The blow snapped the typesetter's head backward spraying blood onto the freshly printed page in the press.

Stryker stepped up and cupped Winslow's ear with his left hand as he circled his right arm back and smashed an elbow into his temple. Stunned, with blood pouring from his mangled nose, Winslow crumpled to his knees. Stryker pushed his head backward, forcing it against the edge of the print machine, and brought the paper cutter down to his throat.

Winslow felt the blade pressing into his flesh. "Please, mister."

"Where is he dammit?"

"I don't . . ." Winslow felt the blade press deeper. "He takes the Powell Street cable car from . . . by the wharf. That's all I know!" He brought his hands to the blade, thought better of it, and dropped them down again. "I sent a message you were looking for him. Said you weren't gonna kill . . . I thought maybe . . ."

Stryker lifted the blade. "I left here with sixty-two dollars. He owes me fifty." He seized Winslow by the front of his shirt and pulled him to his feet. "Get it."

Winslow snatched a rag off the printer press and held it on his still-bleeding nose as he crossed the room to a newspaper lay-out table. Stryker stood behind him with a cocked .44 and Winslow carefully opened the drawer. He pulled out a metal box and fished a key from his pocket to open it. Slowly counting the bills with one hand, he laid them out, leaving the open box on the table.

But Stryker only took the fifty. "Who are the men who followed me?" He demanded, stuffing the money in his shirt pocket.

"Followed you?" Winslow stepped away from the table, allowing Stryker, who ignored the offer, easy access to the remaining cash. "They must be Montel's men. They rob you?"

Stryker headed for the door. He stopped and turned pensively back toward Winslow, who had remained standing by the table. "Would Montel come to your funeral?"

Before the surprised print man could stutter out a reply, Stryker walked out.

After heading one block west on Clay Street to Powell, Stryker hopped on the Powell Street cable car. Much to his disliking, it had already started getting dark. Another reason he didn't care for the city by the bay was shorter, cold and damp days because of rain and fog. He'd lived by Fisherman's Wharf until he was fourteen, when his parents were murdered, but that didn't matter. He preferred the wide open spaces of the American West and to him; the city wasn't part of that.

Two heavily bearded men, dressed like sailors in black Pea Coats, handkerchiefs, and knit caps, scurried to jump on the cable car as it lurched forward up Powell. Stryker took note of them, a tall one and a short skinny one, standing across from the newspaper office when he came out. And he also noticed the same men had crossed the street to walk behind him. They seated themselves opposite him at the far end of the car and glanced his way when spaces opened between other passengers.

Stryker swung down from the cable car before it stopped at the end of the line and ran down Jefferson Street where he darted into an alley. The men shadowing him were caught off guard by Stryker's quick exit. One fought his way through the passengers while the other leapt from the car and ran to the far side. The two nearly collided behind the cable car, then they quickly conferred, and both broke into a jog down the street.

When they reached the alley, one grabbed the sleeve of the other and motioned with his head. "Shorty, go on in there. I'll wait here."

"Piss off Jack." Shorty peered down the darkened passageway and retreated back to the building's corner.

"All right, we both go in," Jack growled.

They entered cautiously, searching likely hiding places along the alley.

They'd gone more than half way when a door burst open behind them. Sharp clicks of a cocking .44 froze them in place.

"Don't turn around!" Stryker stepped into the alley, and jammed the Peacemaker into the back of Jack and ordered, "Tie your partner's arms behind him."

"What with? I ain't got no rope."

"Your belt." Stryker stood in back until the shorter man's arms were tied at the elbows. "Now, pull that handkerchief off his neck and tie it around his wrists. Make it tight."

"Okay, it's tight," Jack said. "Sorry, Shorty." He didn't turn around. Stryker stepped closer and bashed the back of his head with the butt of the gun. Jack collapsed face down to the cobblestones.

Turning to see his partner fall, Shorty snarled, "He's gonna kill you for that."

Stryker knelt and untied the unconscientious man's handkerchief around his neck with one hand while keeping the Peacemaker on Shorty. He shifted the .44 to his left hand and jammed the barrel under the inert man's chin. He then fished the straight razor from his back pocket and dug in the razor's tip an inch below Jack's left ear, drawing it across his throat in one smooth movement. He did it quickly and efficiently, as if he'd done it many times before . . . and he had. The man's throat gapped open in a hideous bloody yawn.

Stryker aimed the gun on Shorty again and stood up.

"You killed him! You . . . you . . . murdered him in cold . . . !"

A cough followed by weak gurgling by Jack caused Shorty to stop in mid-sentence and stare at the dying man.

Stryker wiped the razor with Jack's handkerchief and shoved it in his back pocket. "Turn around."

"You didn't have to kill him. We ain't kilt nobody. I was only kidding 'bout him killing you!"

"What happened to the other man, the one sent to find Montel?" Stryker holstered the Peacemaker and twirled the handkerchief into a long roll.

"We didn't kill him!" Shorty nervously cleared his throat. "We just shanghaied him. That the God's truth, mister." He kept looking back over his shoulder.

"Where's Montel live?"

"On Nob Hill. It's the only one-story house going up the hill. I'll show you!"

Stryker reached around Shorty, jammed the rolled handkerchief into his mouth, and knotted the ends tight behind him.

Stryker pulled the .44 and shoved it in Shorty's back. "Walk." At the alley's end, he grabbed his collar. "Stop."

Stryker spun him around and blasted a knee into Shorty's midsection. The blow doubled him over as Stryker stooped to jam a shoulder into his stomach and heave him over his back. "Keep your mouth shut and stay still if you want to live." He walked out onto the street with his burden, down the hill to the waterfront, and turned right when his boots thudded onto planks. He told the few passersby, the man was drunk.

The evening fog had rolled in with the tide and lights on poles along the waterfront glowed as if swathed in angels hair. Water sloshed against the pilings somewhere in the fog off to Stryker's left, warning him not to wander too far in that direction. A hulking shadow of a ship loomed a few paces ahead. He came to it and stopped.

"Ahoy there!" Stryker's yelled.

"Who's about?"

The reply came from above, signaling Stryker that the man who answered was aboard ship. "What's the name of your ship and where you headed?"

"Euterpe. Who's asking? Wait, I'll come down."

The vague shape of a man at the top of the gangplank became more defined as he walked down. In the meantime, Stryker bent forward and eased Shorty to the ground, patting him on his head as if he were an obedient dog.

"First mate Troms, sir." Upon seeing a man bound and gagged his arm froze in midair and the salute fell away.

"When do you sail and to where?" Stryker asked.

"Midnight sir, with the tide. And we're sailing for New Zealand. Will you be seeking passage sir?"

"No, not me." Stryker hooked a thumb across his shoulder. "This fellow wants to join your crew."

"Ahhh . . . um m m!" Shorty grunted through the handkerchief and shook his head violently from side to side. Stryker gripped his coat collar and twisted.

"You need another man?" Stryker asked.

"Ethan! Patch! Get down here." The first mate called up to the ship.

The two men, who had been leaning on the ship's rail and listening from above, scrambled down to the wharf. One wore a black patch over his eye.

"We've got a fellow here who wants to join our crew. Take him below and make sure he's comfortable." Troms kept his eyes on Stryker as he gave the order.

The air erupted in belly-ripping guffaws as Ethan and Patch clamped onto both of Shorty's tied arms. "Right this way sir," Ethan mocked.

"We've got just the place to make you comfortable," Patch chimed in with more mockery.

The two sailors led the new "crewmember" up the gangplank with the first mate in tow. Stryker turned and strode off toward Hyde Street.

Stryker waited for the Hyde Street cable car crossing Beach Street and then climbed aboard for the ride up to Nob Hill. Had coming back home been a mistake? In fact, although he recognized the names of the streets, he no longer recognized the streets themselves. Home was no longer home, just brick and mortar and strangers. Everyone he once knew in the city was dead. Now, the places he'd known were gone too. An outsider, in an unfamiliar town, that's what he was now.

There's Morgan, though. She's alive and she's a link to . . . to what? He'd met her only a few months ago, and briefly at that. Still, she'd gotten close. The others who did that, died violent deaths. He thought she had as well. The damn jinx made him gun shy. Regardless, he'd signed on to do a job, a well-paying job, and he needed to find the man who lived at the top of the hill.

The surrounding mansions built by founders of the Central Pacific Railroad, including the mostly completed Mark Hopkins mansion, stood at the top of Nob Hill. The single story house wasn't difficult to find. It stood out like a broken tooth in a set of dentures. Being a brick structure with a flat roof, it appeared squat. Montel's house looked like a wart.

Stryker swung down from the cable car before it crested the hill. A light drizzle polished the cobblestones, making them slick, and he nearly slipped. He'd have to adjust to wet streets. A small thing but all the same it irked the mixed-breed. He headed toward Montel's "mansion".

The place had a wrought iron fence, three feet in height, which outlined the quarter acre estate. Stryker pushed through the gate. He came to the front door, rapped a knuckle on it, and was surprised to find it partially open. Draping his right hand on the butt of the Peacemaker, he eased the door wider with the fingers of his free hand.

A startled Miniature French Poodle erupted in a fit of yapping. Stryker's inclination was to pull the Colt and shoot the little bastard, but a woman's shrill whoop changed his mind.

"Phoebe! Now you stop that!" The gray-haired woman in her fifties was so focused on the dog; she didn't notice Stryker at first. When she looked up, she suffered a sharp intake of breath. "Oh!" she exclaimed. "Who are you?" She bent to gather up the still yapping dog and clutched it to her breast. Then she got a second look at the man in the doorway and stepped back.

"Neville Stryker, ma'am. I'm looking for mister Montel. The door was open."

"You just startled me, sorry," she said apologetically. "My name's Gladice. Alain's not here. He asked me to watch Phoebe while he's away."

"Away."

"Yes, you just missed him. He stopped at my house as he left. I live there." She pointed at an elaborate Victorian mansion farther up the hill. "Since he took his house man with him, he asked me to take care of his dog. Said he might be gone a while."

Stryker briefly wondered if the Frenchman attended to her physical needs as well. "Say where he might be going?"

"No, just that he had to leave and take care of business out of the city. I hope he's not gone too long." Gladice hugged Phoebe to her bosom.

No doubt, Stryker figured, the Frenchman scratched her itch. However, he doubted Montel would write and let her know where he was. But the *Examiner* might be more important to Montel.

The newspaper office was dark when he got there and the doors were locked, front and back. The next day's paper couldn't have been printed for distribution by nine-o'clock. Stryker decided not to break in, though, and he walked the remainder of the distance back to the Palace Hotel.

The next morning Winslow told him he hadn't heard from Montel, but he'd decided to continue working the paper. He claimed he'd filled in the editorial column, which Montel always wrote, with human interest stories he made up. Stryker believed him. Perhaps his bandaged nose and blackened eyes made Winslow less inclined to deceive. And besides, Winslow seemed too excited running the paper on his own.

A visit with Ah Toy and Layla proved just as futile. Neither said they'd seen or heard from the Frenchman. Layla offered to entertain him again. "Another time," Stryker said.

A week went by and Stryker still had no clue to Montel's whereabouts.

Stryker wrote a note early one morning, asking for another meeting with the Senator, and gave it to the front desk clerk at the Palace Hotel. He told the young man to deliver it to the Senator, and Stryker glowered at the fellow until he took off with the note. Hearst response came five minutes later.

They met in the same hotel suite. Breakfast was brought up. Both men had steak and eggs with black coffee. "I was afraid the Frenchie would go off and hide somewhere," Hearst said, when Stryker told him Alain Montel had disappeared.

"Winslow, at the newspaper office, doesn't seem to know where he is. The neighbor lady, taking care of his dog, hasn't heard from him, nor has Ah Toy" Stryker added, cutting into the meat.

Hearst raised an eyebrow at the mention of Ah Toy. "Hmmm, Ah Toy has big ears. She'll hear something. I think Winslow will too. Montel's opinion column—he won't give that up." Hearst sipped from his coffee cup and, as if in deep thought, carefully returned the cup to its saucer. "Stryker, tell that man Winslow that he can keep his job with me. But, he's to keep quiet on this."

"Who else might know where he is?" Stryker wanted to know.

Hearst shook his head. "Only played poker with him a few times. Afraid can't help you there."

Stryker swilled the last of the cup's contents down his throat and pushed back from the little table used for breakfast. "Let you know if I hear something." He picked up his hat from the chair where he'd left it and walked out of the Senator's suite without turning back.

CHAPTER FOUR

"**M**ista' Mont'l, how long you say we got stay this 'loom?" Chang Li asked, coming back into the small basement room, his arms loaded with groceries. "I no like ca-wing food ah-way ten block."

Montel chose the below-ground apartment on the corner of Stockton and Pacific streets because it had both front and back doors, with steps leading up to the streets. But it only had one room. Quarters were tight.

"We go soon. I no like smell you body pa'fume," Montel replied, mimicking his Chinese man servant. "I'm preparing a plan–a brilliant plan–I should say." Then he spoke pensively, pacing back and forth in the small room and fingering his goatee. "First," He said, slapping his hands together. "I must have wine and cheese while you prepare the duck."

Not far from San Francisco's Barbary Coast where Montel and his Asian domestic had first holed up, Stryker sat in the Palace Hotel lobby reading the *Examiner*. He'd found two large leather chairs in the corner, separated by a cocktail table where he found the paper someone had left. Sago palms, in thirty-gallon clay pots, walled off the corner, allowing him to isolate himself from the other hotel guests sweeping in and out of the lobby with porters hauling their luggage. Snappy attachés scurried about, attending to their needs. Holding the paper open and in front of him, he kept the curious from gawking at the long-haired man wearing a holstered .44 Peacemaker.

He had no interest in the human interest column Winslow wrote, except to note that it differed from the "evils of capitalism" diatribes which normally filled the space. What few times he'd read the paper since traveling to California, he had noticed the opinion page constantly espoused financial equality. He wouldn't have paid much attention to the writings had not the woman in Egalitaria brought political and philosophical issues to his attention. Musings along those lines hadn't occupied much space in the mind of a man whose sole objective was to survive, often by way of gun and blade.

Skimming across the type, he let his mind drift back to when he first met Morgan Bickford. A damn fine looking woman with high cheekbones, long dark hair parted to one side, narrow waist, and firm breasts. She'd come to his hotel room, stripped naked, and offered her body. Proof that she was willing to do anything for her cause. A simple cause really, the right for a man to keep what he earned. Her body might have been enough, but it was her mind and her principles which persuaded him to help; that, and forty-percent of her property, when recovered and sold. After all, he wouldn't work for free either.

He never collected the money, believing she'd been killed. She lived, though. Maybe he'd try to find her sometime. Yeah, maybe he might just do that.

"Hello Neville."

Stryker lowered the paper. "Hello, Morgan."

She looked even better than he remembered. Her brunette hair was parted on one side and swept back over one ear as she had it in Egalitaria. She wore a white, starched cotton shirt with flap pockets and shoulder epaulets. Her sleeves were rolled to her elbows and she had turned up her collar. The shirt top spread open to reveal tanned skin stretching above her delicate collar bones. A khaki skirt with high-top brown leather boots completed the look. Shit fire, woman. He folded the paper, started to rise.

"No, don't get up. Here." Morgan extended an envelope.

Stryker took it but didn't open it.

"It's a check for sixteen thousand. From Mister Hearst, he bought the mine, and I had him pay forty-percent directly to you," Morgan explained. She side-stepped to the empty chair and seated herself on the front edge of its cushion, hands on her knees, back straight as a board.

"Morgan . . ."

"I know about your deal with Mister Hearst." She stopped him before he could protest. "I recommended you, remember?" She gave him a hint of a smile. "And I know how much he's paying you." The smile faded. "We had a deal, you and me. You kept your part of the bargain. I'll keep mine."

An awkward pause ensued, each waiting for the other to end it. Stryker sat motionless in his chair. Morgan remained rigid in hers.

"Stryker," she began. "West Point, a Major in the artillery, investment banker with the house of Morgan, wanted for murdering the man who caused your wife's death."

Stryker's eyebrow twitched. She, or more likely Hearst, had investigated his past. Sure, Hearst as a Senator, could, and would have, done that before hiring him. He should have known.

"What was her name?"

"Leigh." Stryker said, as if talking to himself, then, more directly to Morgan. "Her name was Leigh."

"I'm sorry."

"A long time ago, Morgan." Stryker's reply surprised him. He suddenly realized with that answer, he was putting his deceased wife in the past. Something he'd never done before. He'd always carried her memory of her with him, in his breast pocket. Now, he struggled with the realization he was letting her fade back in time.

"Mister Stryker." Winslow appeared from out of nowhere next to one of the potted palms.

Stryker and Morgan reluctantly shifted their attention from each other to the man who had interrupted them.

"I got a telegram from Mister Montel. He's in Virginia City . . . in Nevada. Uh, sorry, I inter . . ." Winslow stammered. "He's mailing an opinion article for the paper. And . . . that's all. Sorry." Winslow spun around and left as suddenly as he had appeared.

Both man and woman stared at the other, realizing Stryker would now be heading to Virginia City.

"Hearst asked about you and me." Morgan broke the silence. "I told him . . . most of it anyway. Then he asked me if I would ever marry you."

Stryker's pale gray eyes narrowed.

"I said . . . 'if he asks me.' When you get back from Nevada, I will be here." With that, Morgan rose and walked away.

Stryker awkwardly pushed himself out of the chair as she left.

CHAPTER FIVE

Winslow glanced up from his work and saw Stryker through the window, on his way toward the newspaper office. He opened the door ahead of him.

"The telegram is here on the desk." Winslow quickly turned away from the opened door and took the eight steps to retrieve the letter before Stryker got inside.

"I kept it so you could see it. There, on top, 'Virginia City'." Winslow held the yellow Western Union telegram out to Stryker and pointed at the origination office on it. The telegram said, "WILL MAILWEEKLY COLUMNS. ALAIN."

"I guess he didn't think I would tell you. But, you would know anyway when you saw them in the paper," Winslow said, somewhat apologetically.

Stryker left the newspaper office without telling Winslow of his plans to travel to Nevada. He figured Winslow might tell Montel, but then again, he might not. Winslow liked the new freedom of running the paper, except now he had to do Alain's opinion page once a week.

Stryker made his way to the Bank of California where he opened an account, and deposited the check. He named Morgan as beneficiary. Next, he went back to the Palace Hotel. There, he made arrangements with a hotel valet to buy a train ticket to Reno, leaving from San Francisco in four hours. The helpful valet informed him he could also travel by rail on the Virginia Truckee line from Reno to Virginia City. Both tickets would be at the Ferry House ticket window. The roan was to be delivered there as well. The valet hurried off to complete the tasks. Travel arrangements secured, Stryker gathered his belongings from the room and checked out of the Palace.

Once the ferry brought the rail cars east of the bay, it would take a day over the Sierras to reach Reno. There was a good chance he could be in Virginia City in thirty-six hours.

Stryker rode the cable car to the large wooden Ferry House where, down the street to his right, he saw the big roan horse being led to the station. He picked up the tickets and went inside. There was a food shop, crowded with would-be passengers, and he saw that he'd have a long wait for a biscuit and a cup of coffee. No problem, he thought, he still had two and half hours until the train left.

Coffee that the counter waitress poured in the heavy, cream-colored mug was fresh, strong, and good. Hot steam escaped from the homemade biscuit when he cut it open. He leaned against a wooden shelf which ran along the wall to enjoy both. The cool damp air from outside rushed in through the doors to battle the shop's aroma of coffee and baked goods. Each time the doors closed, the inside warmth overwhelmed the cool isolated pockets and the café air hung heavy and somewhat steamy.

Almost all the men in the place wore suits and derby hats, looking their dandified best. The women, vested in their finery with hats and parasols, acquitted themselves even more so. Stryker, looking around at all the passengers while he munched on the biscuit, wondered if he be would boarding a train bound to some special occasion. Even an exceptionally tall man of color, a man standing a good three inches taller than Stryker, outfitted himself in a suit, minus the derby. It took a few minutes to realize it wasn't the suit so much, nor the way he comported himself, that made the tall black man so striking. Rather, it was the copy of the *Examiner* stuffed between his arm and body which caught Stryker's eye. The man could read. Stryker, as a teenager, had fought with men like him on the union side in the war. Negroes, most of them brave in battle, bled red too, and they had earned his respect. But none of the ones he'd known could read.

Stryker finished eating the biscuit and drained the rest of the coffee while it was still warm. He'd taken his time, content with measured consumption, as he let his eyes wander around the room, stopping to linger on a few with a casual interest. Many of the men who passed him went out of their way not to make eye contact with the steely-eyed mixed-breed whose mouth seemed to form a snarl each time he bit into the biscuit. Most of the women did likewise. A couple, more of the venturesome ones, flashed beguiling looks his way, as if daring him to introduce himself. However, his fierce countenance remained the same, so the two women abruptly abandoned their delusions and stared straight ahead as they walked by him. He decided to go see about his horse.

Stryker left the café and walked down a corridor leading out to the piers where he found train cars, freight and passengers, lined up on tracks awaiting the ferry boat. Off to the right, he saw the red roan, already saddled, in a holding pen with two other horses. It shook its mane and whinnied a greeting as Stryker approached.

"I suppose I don't have to ask if he's your horse," the young corral attendant said.

"Got a claim ticket for him," Stryker said. He intended to get the Winchester from its boot.

"His word's good enough for me." The boy smiled.

The horse nuzzled Stryker's chest as he ran his hands down its neck and then down both legs, checking for areas of tenderness. After lifting and inspecting each front hoof, he moved to the back legs. Satisfied the Army had properly groomed and cared for his horse, he secured the worn carpet bag holding a clean shirt and personal belongings to the saddle horn. He pulled the carbine from the scabbard, held it in both hands, judging rounds in magazine tube by the gun's weight. It felt heavy enough to be nearly full (ten) of the big .44-40 rounds. Then, he shoved it back in the boot. He came around front of the roan. "Which car you loading him?"

"That first line there," the young man answered, gesturing in the direction of two passenger cars with three freight cars behind them. The engine, hooked backwards to the last freight car, stood ready to push the cars onto the ferry. "You going to Reno, right?" He paused for a confirming nod from Stryker. "He'll go in the last car there," he said pointing. "They put livestock in the rear."

Stryker, satisfied with the roan's transport, strolled along the pier looking for a bench. He found a wooden one on the edge of the latest landfill effort. There he watched wagons loaded with dirt and garbage roll to the water's edge where men shoveled the fill out. He momentarily wondered if the stink would always remain, and but then shifted his attention to ships by the piers and those anchored out in the bay. There must be hundreds, he guessed, with their empty masts pricking skyward, stirring the air as gentle swells rocked the ships.

The money interrupted his thoughts. If he were successful in getting the newspaper signed over to Hearst, he could live a life of leisure. He imagined a life of leisure, suddenly a shudder coursed through him. Him, going to performances? Eating fancy dinners? And . . . and doing what? Sitting in an overstuffed chair getting fat? Don't think so. He'd lived his life on the edge. A dangerous life to be sure, but at least he lived while alive. And he lived alone. No schedules and no one told him what to do. And this Morgan woman, she won't sit on her ass. What would he do, follow her around the mines like a damn lap dog? Having a woman work while he "lived a life of leisure" didn't sit well with him.

Ah, hell, he'd have to sort those things out later. First, he had to find Montel, get him to sign the document in his pocket, or maybe just kill him. Thinking about a life with money darkened his mood.

He spied the paddlewheel ferry approaching from a quarter mile away. He noticed how low the sun had sunk behind him and he rose to head inside the Ferry House to locate the Oakland gate. The mob at the gate surprised him. Hundreds, maybe even a thousand waiting passengers crowded against the boarding gate, so that even a well-armed, ill-tempered man wouldn't be able to push his way through the mass of people. So he stood at the rear, and soon hundreds more stacked up behind him.

A half hour later, the last off-boarding passengers came through the exit gate and the train engine, cars attached, rolled onto the ferry remarkably quickly. Then, the boarding gate, which he couldn't see, opened, allowing the mass of people to shuffle forward. Bumping, jostling, and shoving one another, they pushed ahead, as if afraid the gate would close, cutting them off before they could board. Several times men and women shoved hard into him, offering apologies, then melting away into the crowd.

The tall black man brushed by Stryker, the same one as in the café. He reached over another man's shoulder in front and grabbed a young woman by the hair.

He pulled her back viciously, knocking the man behind her out of the way. "Give it back." He ordered, his voice, deep and gravelly.

The crowd opened up a six-foot space around them, but they were pushed forward from behind. The girl gripped his massive wrists with both her hands and grunted like an animal, gritting her teeth in pain and anger.

He twisted harder.

The girl screamed, her pain so great she could no longer resist. "Here!" She sobbed. "Take it!" She let one hand go, dug inside her coat, and pulled out a leather billfold.

He grabbed the billfold and released her hair. The girl fought her way through the crowd and disappeared. Stryker had been attempting to pass with the crowd, but the Negro gripped him by the shoulder, and said, "it's yours mister. She took it."

Stryker, then for the first time, recognized that the wallet the huge man held out to him was his. He took the billfold and looked in the direction the pickpocket had fled.

"Let her go. She'll get her due someday, and learn payback is hell."

"Reckon I owe you," Stryker allowed. He pinched out a five-dollar note.

The big man shook his head. "A beer's 'bout right."

Minutes later, they stood at one of several bars on the ferry, this one on the second level, had mirrors hanging behind the mahogany bar, and large rectangular windows stretching along a side wall. It had turned to late afternoon, late enough for the bar drinkers to be standing six deep. However, Stryker and the tall black giant easily pushed their way to the counter. Sloshing their beers back through thirsty would-be drinkers who were elbowing their own way to bar, they stepped outside and found an empty section of railing to lean on.

"Why?"

"Why'd I help you?" The black man replied, sipping the foamed beer. "Name's Ivory, Ivory T. Naismith." He did not extend his hand. After seeing Stryker's eyebrow twitch, he added, "I don't know. I suppose my folks thought it'd be funny. Well, I'm a Quaker, became one when I attended Lincoln University. Quakers ran the place." He paused. "It only seemed right. She stole your money."

Stryker raised his beer glass, blew some of the foam off, and took a gulp.

"Where you headed mister . . . ?"

"Virginia City," Stryker answered.

"You don't look like a miner," Ivory said, noticing the Peacemaker slung low off Stryker's hip. "Isn't the silver playing out there anyway, mister . . . ?"

"Stryker," Stryker answered curtly. Guess the beer's not good enough he figured, looking out over the bay. Facing Ivory again, "Didn't know Quakers drank."

"Only by ourselves." The big man smiled.

For a moment Stryker wondered if Ivory got his name from the wide toothy grin, but then quickly realized a newborn wouldn't have had any teeth.

"I'm going there myself," Ivory said, referring to Virginia City. "My employer is sending me there to analyze ore, and then I'm heading to Park City. You staying long in Virginia City?"

"No. Business. Shouldn't take long. Where's Park City?" Stryker hoped it was far away.

"Northern Utah. Big silver mines there too."

Stryker finished the beer faster than he really wanted. "Good luck, Ivory." The big man seemed alright. Stryker fought with darkies who had acquitted themselves well in the war, only to be ignored later by both the North and South. And then, they damn near starved to death. This Ivory, though, had made something of himself.

He pushed from the rail and ambled back inside the bar. After putting the empty glass on a table, he wove his way between clumps of drinkers to an opposite doorway, and sought out a uniformed crewman who could tell him when and where to board the Nevada train. By the time the ferry docked at the Oakland Pier, nighttime had fully arrived, and Stryker learned the train didn't depart until 11:10 the next morning. He had a choice; sleep in the first class cabin he'd already paid for or bunk with the roan. He checked on the horse and slept in the cabin. After all, there are some things for which money comes in handy.

The following morning, Stryker set out to find a place to eat breakfast. They served it in the dining car, but Stryker figured he'd be on the train long enough, and had steak and eggs in the Crown Hotel instead. Inside, a small nook off the lobby served as a dining area for hotel guests and he paid an extra dollar for the meal. He picked up the *Examiner* left there by another diner from the next table, and read it as he ate.

Headlines told of the latest scandal concerning a city official's bribery, another recounted the verbal joisting between two politicians vying for the San Francisco mayoral office, and so on, and so on. Then, the *Opinion* piece on page four by Alain Montel caught his eye.

ROBBER BARONS ROB US ALL *By Alain Montel*

A small group of powerful gangsters here in California and across this great land control the majority of wealth, most of it ill-gotten. These gangsters don't break kneecaps, but they destroy people's lives all the same. They wear three-piece suits and you'll find them in their mansions on Nob Hill, dining in the finest restaurants, or attending the most opulent galas impeccably festooned in tuxedos with long tails. And, they amass their huge sums of wealth by walking across the bent backs of the rest of us.

By exerting control over natural resources, influencing crooked politicians, creating monopolies to raise prices, and paying pitifully low wages to workers who slave for them, these rich businessmen selfishly reap huge fortunes by exploiting American working families, children, elderly, and the poor. Big money, they use it to stay in power. Government doesn't control Wall Street. Wall Street controls government. You'll see the likes of rail executives, bankers, and industrialists rubbing elbows with United States Senators, Congressmen, Mayors, and other government officials. What is the glue that binds together this chamber of crooked bedfellows? Money, and lots of it.

Citizens of San Francisco, of America, we must declare a moral and political war against the millionaires, the powerful, and the politicians they've corrupted. We must stand united for truth and justice. Together we can win. And we must do whatever it takes to right the wrongs committed against us.

Fight! Fight! If we must, we'll take to the streets. Rally to the cause! Join us! Win with us!

Two and a half hours passed and Stryker sat in a Central Pacific coach car watching the California landscape crawl by, thinking about Montel's writing. His private cabin had no chairs, just two sleeping berths, and he'd come forward to find a seat by a window. The train had rolled south around Mount Diablo and was now running northwest toward Stockton. The tracks ran north, west of Stockton and Sacramento, before turning east and over the Sierra's to Reno. So far, the land was fairly flat, but when the tracks curved, he could see the high mountains ahead looming in the distance.

Stryker thought, if he hadn't seen how Montel's type of rhetoric could destroy a town, he would have been moved to act in support of the Frenchman's column. It had been Morgan's town, hers and her husband's, Bickford, named after them. That is, until Norwood and his gang, took it over and renamed it Egalitaria. They killed Morgan's husband and took their mine and ranch, redistributing the profits equally, supposedly. Well, as it turned out, some were more equal than others. And, it didn't matter how hard you worked, you still got equal pay. They said it was equal, anyway. Workers and miners began to work less, and why not? You still got the same as everyone else. Eventually, production ground down to almost nothing and work had to get done at the point of a gun. That's when he, Stryker, wandered into town looking for his stolen horse, and Morgan offered her body and forty-percent of her property for his help.

The citizens of Egalitaria finally realized they were worse off under Norwood than before. The Bickfords hadn't worked them as forced labor. Sure, at times, the workers felt exploited, and they might have been, but at least they had a choice on whether to work or move on.

Besides the worker's plight, there was another problem with Montel's scheme. Who would step up and start a business, a factory, or a railroad, if there were no profits for the owners? The train which Stryker now rode—who would have built it?

Stryker sat by the window, running these thoughts through his head. So, it seemed, getting the *Examiner* was more than just collecting on a bet for Hearst. Because of the politics of it, he suspected Morgan had a hand in this. So what? It didn't matter. If he killed two or three birds with the same stone, or bullet, fine.

That damn woman was like a headstrong horse. If he ended up with her, she'd have to be taken well-in-hand early. The corner of Stryker's mouth twitched. He'd taken her well-in-hand when they first met.

Mid-afternoon and the Central Pacific had chugged past Stockton and Sacramento, with brief stops in each. Stryker watched the terrain through the window gradually shift from flat ground to grassy rolling hills, then to tree-covered hills, mostly pine, with clumps of deciduous trees surrounded by the evergreens. The Shea locomotive and the five helper engines added at the last stop started to strain on steepening grades, now coming more often.

Stryker sat by himself. His fierce countenance kept other riders from taking a seat next to him. Men in business suits, whom he'd seen clustered in groups with other cigar-smoking men at the San Francisco station, had rejoined their delicate halves in the coach. Small children accompanied two couples. Two women, apparently a mother and grandmother, constantly fussing over a baby, thankfully sat in back, taking up the entire bench. The three unaccompanied men chose to sit by the couples, near the women if possible.

"Mister Stryker." Ivory scooted in beside Stryker.

"Ivory," Stryker replied, pulling his bag a little closer.

"These are the Sierras ahead?" The big black hulk of a man leaned over to peer out the window at the rising landscape.

"That's them."

"I've read about them. Lots of gold found in those hills. Been studying geological maps in my cabin, what maps there are. Hasn't been fully mapped, these mountains. Decided to come see for myself."

"Lots of men died trying to get it," Stryker added dryly.

"Dying ain't livin'."

Stryker glanced sideways at Ivory.

"There were several of us students philosophizing as only drunks can do at three in the morning. Jerry, his name was Jerry, after sipping what must have been his twelfth beer, belched and offered that little gem. He also said 'we ain't getting 'outta this thing alive."

"A real Aristotle, your Jerry,"

"Yes, he was. A jealous husband shot him the following year. You're a learned man?"

Stryker thought for a moment. Why should he tell this man anything about himself? What the hell, "West Point."

"No sh . . . . Hey, why's the train stopping?" Ivory craned his neck toward the window. "Something's happening. The hill isn't that . . . stee . . . Hey!"

Stryker gripped both hands on the bench-back in front of him and powered his body around Ivory into the aisle. In two quick steps, he was at the rear door. He threw open the door, pulled the Colt, and knelt on one knee. Ivory leapt to his feet, stumbled over Stryker after one long step, and fell on him.

"Sorry, Mister Stryker!" Ivory grunted.

Stryker was struggling to get his feet under him when Ivory placed his huge hands against Stryker's back to push himself up. The added weight caught Stryker by surprise and his arms collapsed. Both men crashed to the floor again. By then, several more of the men crowded into the doorway. They did their best not to step on the two fallen men, but more passengers behind them shoved forward, and Stryker got flattened a third time. Pushing hard, he rolled to his right and heaved Ivory off to one side. He jammed the barrel of the six-gun between Ivory's pearly whites and thumbed the hammer back.

The big man scrunched his face and shut his eyes, waiting for the bullet.

"Everybody out! Hands in the air!" A shout came from outside the train.

"Gol-dammit, they're robbing the train!" One of the men inside, looking out a window yelled the warning.

Stryker viciously jerked the barrel from Ivory's mouth, chipping two teeth with the front sight blade. He pushed away from the big man and finally made it to his feet. Ivory fought his way up as well, throwing another man off him as he rose. Stryker and Ivory shoved their way through passengers, now scrambling away from the door to peer anxiously out the windows.

Outside, six heavily-armed men, stood in a clearing in front of the pines, and each had a Winchester Repeater pointed at the coach windows. Four wore ragged short brim hats, scruffy coats, and well-worn pants. Stryker guessed the narrow brim hats to be out of work miners. The other three wore Stetsons and clothing which suggested they stayed above ground. All wore handkerchiefs over their faces. Stryker counted no more than the six, but figured others would likely be up at the engine. Then, the engineer came down the track with another robber behind him. Stryker aimed the Peacemaker at the man he figured to be the gang's leader.

"No, Stryker," Ivory said. The words whistled through his broken teeth. "There's women and children in here." His huge brown hand pressed down on the gun barrel.

"Come out with your hands up and nobody gets hurt!" The man gang leader yelled. The man to his left could be younger, maybe late teens, but it was hard to tell with his face covered. The young robber anxiously jacked a round in his carbine, needlessly ejecting a live round. Stryker thought he heard him giggle.

The train conductor appeared at the coach door. "We better do what they say. They felled a tree on the track. Everyone raise your hands and follow me." He paused. "Please, everyone go out this door." He raised his hands and turned to move away from the doorway. Slowly, placing each foot ahead of the other, he stepped down from the train car. And then, one by one, the passengers, with raised arms, filed out the door and off the train.

Up ahead the Shay puffed blasts of steam as if frustrated at the log in its way.

"Come on, Stryker." Ivory raised his hands, dragging them against the ceiling as he joined the other passengers shuffling out the door.

"Well, God-Almighty. Look who we have here," The robber to the right of the leader said. "A big buck nigger."

"Easy, boys. We don't want no trouble, do we?" The gang leader saw Stryker coming out last and spied the Colt still holstered on his hip. "You mister, you need to unbuckle that gun belt. Lon, you and Berni go slide open the door on that car." He pointed at the express car. "You two dammit!" He jabbed a finger at two of the short brims when no one moved.

Stryker figured they weren't using their real names. His fingers slowly worked the knot on the leather string tied around his thigh.

"Hurry boys. This train has a schedule to keep." The leader waved his carbine at the passengers. "You folks just empty them pockets on the ground, and step back, and face the train. Don't be holdin' nuthin'back. Hey you!" He pointed his gun at Stryker. "Hurry up with that gun belt."

Lon and Bernie struggled with the heavy, wooden sliding door. The express car's floor was chest high to the two men standing on the rail ties, and the door rolled along a track secured at the top. Usually, the door would be maneuvered from a station platform or from inside the car, but standing on the ground and pushing from the bottom caused the door to bind.

"C'mon you two." The gang leader watched as Lon and Berni strained to slide the door open.

"Hey, maybe it's locked up, on the inside," Lon yelled out. Then it began to roll.

"There it goes," Berni shouted excitedly.

Both men grunted loudly and gave a mighty shove. The door finally rolled open. They eagerly peeked inside the darkened interior.

Four shotgun blasts greeted them.

Lon took a blast in his handkerchief and was killed instantly with the handkerchief stapled into his face. Berni took the other three blasts in his throat, blowing most of it away. A single string of sinew and fractured vertebrae held the head that now hung upside-down, on his back. Even with the gruesome injury, he managed one step backward before he fell.

Pumping their carbine levers furiously, the three men in Stetsons fired at the express car after Lon and Berni were killed.

All the passengers except Stryker and an old woman had thrown themselves to the ground when the shotguns blasted. Stryker dove to his right, away from the passengers, pulling the Colt, and fired two quick bullets, one into the gang leader's chest and one in the belly of the robber next to him. Both men were still sending a fusillade of shots into the express car's interior when Stryker's rounds angrily tore into their torsos. Stryker hit the dirt, rolled to a prone position, and fired a third shot at the giggler. The round caught the man high in the chest.

The engineer flung himself to the ground beside the passengers, and the two remaining miners nervously raked their guns back and forth. They glanced at each other, evidently trying to decide what to do. Then, all at once, they spun around and scrambled under the tender car. By the time Stryker could sight the Peacemaker on them, they'd disappeared to the other side of the train. He heard them running up the track.

Ivory rose from the ground first and, one by one, the rest of the passengers got to their feet, dusting themselves off as they began to find their voices. Stryker lay on the ground, ready to fire another round if needed.

"I need a doctor." The gut shot robber lay curled on his side, clutching his stomach. He pulled the handkerchief down to his neck. His clean-shaven face was contorted in pain. Blood flowed between his fingers, pooling in the dirt. "Please, I need a doctor," he repeated through clenched teeth.

Ivory stopped slapping the dust off his clothes and quick-stepped to the injured robber. He gently pulled the man's bloody hand away to inspect the wound.

Stryker, satisfied the other robbers were either dead or gone, got to his feet, and approached Ivory by the wounded man. He tapped Ivory on the shoulder and held out the Colt in the palm of his hand.

"No, Stryker. Just because he called me names, doesn't mean I should shoot him."

Stryker flipped the gun in his hand and fired. The bullet hit the robber in the temple. "Get on the train, Ivory."

The Pinkerton men poured out of the train and surveyed the scene following the last shot. A few minutes later, the engineer and brakeman used two of the would-be robber's horses to drag the log from the tracks. They planned to bury all three dead men in a shallow grave and ride along the tracks back toward Alta, trailing five horses behind the two they'd ride. Another train came through Alta in eight hours. The other two Pinkerton men still guarding the express car would wait for them in Reno.

Stryker climbed aboard the coach, and settled in the only available seat, next to Ivory. He'd been delayed outside by the Pinkerton men who wanted to talk about the attempted robbery, hinting they might have a job for him. The passengers viewed him differently. Although the males simply got on the train and re-took their seats, three of the women spoke to Stryker after the Pinkerton agents walked away. He dropped his foot back off the first step and faced the women

"We suppose we should thank you for stopping the robbery, you and those other men on the train," the woman who stood a head taller and fifty pounds heavier than her two friends, said. She had huge breasts and she carried them as though they somehow made up for her large girth. The other two women nodded in agreement. "You're obviously good with guns. You're a gunfighter, a killer. The way you shot that injured man proves it. He was helpless." The lady's words were accompanied by more head wagging from the two women. "You see mister, whatever your name is, we've been robbed on this train before, and it's always been peaceful. No one's been hurt."

One of the other women wearing a floral dress added, "No one's been hurt."

"They rob the safe," the big woman went on. "And they line us up outside the train and we throw a little money on the ground for them to take. The men do anyway. We give them trinkets."

"We know better than to wear good jewelry," the floral-dressed women said, as if to imply good jewelry wasn't fashionable during train robberies.

Stryker wondered if these women fancied romance with the robbers while in bed with their husbands. "Ever give them your underwear?"

"Insulted, or perhaps not, the three acted like it, and hurried away to board the train. Stryker heard one laugh as she stepped on.

The train rolled down a half mile to level ground, and chugged back up the hill past two Pinkerton men left behind to bury the dead.

CHAPTER SIX

The train wound up through California Oak, Digger Pine, Ponderosa Pine, Laurel, Chinquapin, and various types of brush, climbing steadily, but with few grades much over two per cent. The travelers were still in the Sierra foothills, and yet they'd rolled over several trestles. Thirteen tunnels lay ahead.

"Why did you shoot him?" Ivory asked. The sun had sat behind them and passengers began to see their own reflections in the window glass instead of the darkening landscape outside. The train passed through two tunnels and over several trestles before Ivory broke the silence. He'd sat staring out the window. Stryker, with the brim of his Stetson lowered to brow level, didn't invite conversation. "Stryker, why'd you just kill him?"

Stryker answered under his hat. "They don't get a second chance."

"To what? Come after us, you?"

"You're big target Ivory, a big black one. Two of their men got their heads blown off, they'd a shot somebody before running."

'So this is the wild west," Ivory said to himself, attempting to see through his reflection in the widow. He sat silent for several long minutes, looking out the window, and thinking. After a while he settled back on the seat, and turned to the mixed-breed, who still sat with the hat tilted down, and his arms crossed. "You're damn good with that gun."

Stryker tipped the brim up with a forefinger. "If there's another robbery, have the women drop their panties on the ground." He got to his feet and left.

"Say, what?" Ivory whistled through chipped teeth, but it had taken too long for Stryker's words to sink in and he was out the door.

On the way to his sleeper berth, Stryker grabbed a mug of coffee, a biscuit, and picked up a paper heralding Lillie Langtry coming to Piper's Opera House in Virginia City. Too late to read, he laid it aside for a morning read with breakfast.

Stryker slept fitfully, tormented with nightmares of Leigh. The same damn dream that invaded his subconscious all too often, usually when he couldn't sink into a deep sleep, and he couldn't tonight. The artillery shell blew fragments of shrapnel ripping through her, leaving her body broken and bleeding. He found her like that, helpless to save her; and knowing he was partially responsible for the round that landed out of sector. She died in his arms, his name on her lips. The train wheels clacked relentlessly. His consciousness rose to the surface when he heard them and they carried, dragged him along, but not far enough away from the haunting dreams.

Thankfully, after long restless hours, the dark night outside the train turned to gray. Resigned to another loss of a good night's sleep, Stryker roused himself from bed. Truckee, that's what the conductor called, passing Stryker's door. They'd gone through Donner's Pass during the night and now the small town of Reno lay not more than one hour ahead. From there, he'd transfer to the Virginia-Truckee Line, a narrow gauge track, and complete the last leg of the trip to Virginia City. Now, for the first time, he began to consider the options, forming a plan to find Montel. Landing in town and asking around for the Frenchman would be too obvious, possibly alerting Montel, driving him into hiding to leave town. Stryker ran these likelihoods through his mind, as he dressed. The coach car in which he sat had begun the trip with the perfumed cleanliness of humanity. However, after a full day and night, the car just carried humanity. So, after a biscuit and sausage, he returned to the sleeper where he sat alone and drank a second cup of coffee.

"Reno." The conductor's call came quicker than Stryker expected. He opened the window and looked out at the sparse buildings. Not much of a town, he thought.

Reno presented an hour's wait for the train to Virginia City, time to haul out the roan, scout the buildings that had sprung up after the transcontinental railroad and the Comstock Lode made the Reno junction of about three-thousand people more important, and talk to Ivory. He found him having a beer at a watering hole on Virginia Street, a single-story wooden building with a bar in front and a card room in back. The sign above the door read "Liquor in the Front and Poker in the Rear." Other than that it had no name.

'Mister Stryker." Ivory spied the mixed-breed's reflection in the mirror behind the bar and turned around. "Buy you a beer?"

"Buy my own." Stryker replied, slapping coins on the bar. The bartender sloshed a glass of heavily foamed brew down on the countertop. Stryker picked it up and took a sip. "I want to talk to you." He guided them to a table in the corner of the saloon.

"Looking for a man in Virginia City," Stryker began. Need him to sign a paper, a deed, to property he owes a man. I need to find him before he runs again. Figure if we're together while I look for him, it'll be easier. You do your business. I'll do mine."

"You gonna kill 'im?"

"I'm collecting on a debt."

"All legal, I suppose?"

Stryker nodded.

"Hmmm." Ivory rubbed his chin. "This man you're colleting for, he in San Francisco?"

Stryker nodded.

"Mine too" Ivory said. "I mean who I work for. He's in San Francisco, fellow named Hearst. May be easier for me too. I can carry a lot of valuable ore with me at times. Seeing you with me might make a man think twice about robbing me." Then he asked, "what if you complete your business before I leave Virginia City?"

"We leave at the same time." Stryker decided not to tell Ivory they worked for the same man, not just yet anyway.

"Ever been down a mine shaft?" Ivory asked.

"No."

"Tunnels go down to hell itself. You'll like them."

Stryker finished the beer in one long swallow and plopped the empty glass on the table with an air of finality. He scraped the wooden chair away from the table as if to stand and leave. He hesitated. Then, he gripped the front of the chair seat between his knees, and brought it under the table again. "You been to Virginia City before?"

"Once, about four years ago. What about you?"

"Yes. You know anyone?"

No, only there a few days. I worked with an assay man who got shot dead on the Ophir. Well, there is a woman at the Silver Queen Hotel, *was* there anyway—she might be gone now, too. She was curious about the rumors, if you know what I mean."

"It's more important to keep her mouth shut than her legs. That goes for your mouth too. Say nothing about why I'm here, Ivory."

"If she's still in town, which I doubt, since the Lode's 'bout played out, you're a guard my employer sent with me on this trip, that do?"

This time Stryker scooted the chair back, stood, and walked out of the crudely named saloon. He stood on the boardwalk and surveyed the street. Reno was warming up. The morning temperature marched toward the 90's, and would get there by mid-afternoon. He hoped to be in Virginia City before that, where the air would be ten degrees cooler at 6,100 feet.

When he returned to the train station, the Virginia-Truckee was crawling down from the low hills west of Reno, blowing black smoke into a blue sky three miles in the distance. Next to the station platform, the roan stood saddled in a small loading pen with four mules, waiting to be led up a ramp onto the stock car. He inquired about his carry bag and found it loaded on the baggage cart. He fished the train ticket from his pocket and waited.

After hopping onto the station platform to stand beside Stryker, Ivory asked, "Did you know Virginia City has, or had, over one-hundred saloons?"

Stryker remained focused on the approaching train. Occasionally, he'd let his eyes settle on the waiting passengers, their numbers increasing as the train got closer. He heard Ivory. He just ignored him.

"Took a lot of spring water to wash the mine dust outta their throats," Ivory added when he got no response from the stoic mixed-breed.

"Virginia City," the conductor called as he passed through the coach. He mumbled it, actually, as if one could tell his tired greeting announced a tired town.

Stryker's first impression, seeing the many stores and saloons boarded up, was . . . the boom was over. There were still a good many people in Virginia City, which had sprung to life, like over twenty other towns around the Comstock, but the good times were ending. At one time the Lode produced most of the silver in the world with twenty-five thousand people living and working in Virginia City– not any more. Stryker thought the town reminded him of an aging romance. The love making begins exciting and wonderful, maybe even great. And then, after a while it fades to so, so. Virginia City looked so, so. "Pretty fucked out," he whispered to himself.

"How's that?" Ivory asked, also noticing a drastic change from his prior visit.

"Nothing."

"I stayed at the Silver Queen, last I was here. Okay for you?"

Stryker nodded and spun on his heels. "Gonna tend to the horse."

"The Queen's on C' Street, a few blocks from the station, and up the hill." Ivory couldn't tell if Stryker heard him.

Stryker walked the roan a half hour, stabled him, and arranged for feed and water with a cripple who'd had his foot crushed by an ore cart. Afterwards, he headed up to the Silver Queen, passing a saloon on C Street along the way with the gruesome name, "Bucket of Blood". The Piper Opera House stood behind the Queen, making it easy to catch a performance, if he should choose not to throw down drinks every night at the "Bucket". Surveying the town as he walked, Stryker thought it wasn't really dead, or even close to it. But Virginia City had to work awfully hard to stay alive.

Ivory sat in the garishly appointed hotel bar, complete with red velvet wallpaper, lots of brass, mahogany paneling, and a painting of a pale-skinned, naked red headed woman, with bright red nipples protruding from full and firm breasts. The barroom boasted bawdy.

"Got a room on the top floor. Check in's that way." Ivory pointed with a near-empty beer glass.

Stryker procured a room on the second floor, and then joined Ivory, nursing his third beer at a bar table. "What's next Ivory?"

"Right now, I'm gonna finish this beer while I wait for my equipment to be brought over to the Comstock Assay Office. Then . . . I'll mosey over and open the crates. How about you, Mister Gunfighter?"

"Remember, I'm your damn guard, Ivory," Stryker growled, irritated at the prospect of his mission being compromised by a tongue soaked in alcohol. "Why don't you "mosey" over to the assay office now?" Stryker asked sarcastically. "I've got some looking around to do." He had a hunch the Frenchie would have acquainted himself with the "painted ladies" of Virginia City.

"I'll have another beer or two first." Bristling at the mixed-breed's sarcasm, Ivory saluted with the beer glass,

"Wouldn't want to do it, but I will." Stryker's eyes narrowed to silver slits.

The two men stared hard at one another, tension building.

"You big boys new in town?" Buela, a tall woman, looking quite slim in a long, purple-satin dress with its high stiff collar, draped an arm around Ivory's shoulder. She had worried eyes, but she was still more attractive now than when she had been young and pretty. "This town's got three-hundred courtesans on the welcoming committee. Make you glad you came here." She flashed a beguiling smile.

"Three-hundred!" Ivory seemed impressed.

"You get many foreigners?" Stryker asked.

"Chinese, of course, because of the railroad. The miners went union, four dollars a day, so mostly whites from here and Europe work the mines. But we have girls for all. I mean all," Buela replied, her voice a little edgy after being pushed off topic. She got back on point. "Even for you." She smiled at Ivory and ran her hand up and down his upper arm. "Tell them Buela sent you."

"Europeans come all the way here to work the mines?" Stryker pressed on. "Who are your best customers? Germans, British, French, Spanish?"

"You writing a book?" Buela grew more exasperated.

"In fact, I am," Stryker said to Buela and Ivory's raised eyebrows. "Tell me about yourself, and I want to hear about your girls' past, about your lives before you came here. I'd like to write and tell my readers real stories of your hardships, your kindness, and you know... soiled doves with hearts of gold, that kind of thing."

Buela's features changed abruptly. Suddenly gone was the put-on expression of a saleswoman. Gone and replaced with a heavy veil of sorrow. The woman pulled away from Ivory and left. To Stryker's surprise, she returned a few minutes later with two shot glasses filled with good bourbon. Buela placed one on the table for him, and the other in front of an empty chair next to Stryker. She sat down, took a long sip, and carefully placed the bourbon on the table. She studied the glass momentarily, spinning it slowly between her hands. Then she looked up and asked, "What would you like to know?"

Sensing Buela wanted to vent her soul, Stryker decided not to delay her by asking for pen and paper. "What brought you here, Buela?"

She told him she'd come from Louisiana with her husband, and that they'd acquired part interest in a mine. He'd died in a cave-in. The other partners told her the mine was worthless and they bought her out for pennies on the dollar. A favor to her husband, they'd said. The mine produced millions. She spent all the money on lawyers trying to recover her mine interest, but the lawyers were shady, friends of the other partners. She had no money for a ticket back home, so she started as a saloon girl. Soon, she discovered she could make more money caring for miner's physical needs than she could by getting them drunk. Lots of it.

She'd been pregnant twice, she told Stryker. The first child was born dead. The second one lived until the father, a well-known member of the community, married with children of his own, drowned the baby in a wash basin. Buela later learned she'd had a little girl. She still had dreams of her, nightmares really. The dead girl aged in the dreams as though she had lived, and in them, the girl would be running toward Buela with outstretched arms.

Ivory got up from the table and came back with two more whiskeys. "Here, I'll go check my equipment."

Finally, after a long hour evincing her lamentable past, Buela said she could no longer accommodate men, except with her hands.

49

She had a sickness down "there", she'd said, sounding apologetic. So she referred most of 'em now. She made enough to pay for room and board. Taking a long, labored breath, she paused.

"Buela, I'm not a writer," Stryker said.

"I know that. I want you to kill the father."

CHAPTER SEVEN

They cut a deal.

Stryker learned from Buela there were five or six French speaking men in Virginia City. She thought three had shown up in the last two months, but the name Alain Montel wasn't familiar to her. However, she would try to find out if any of them had recently arrived from San Francisco.

Franklin Jefferson, a good looking man, had a pretty wife named Jezebel and two attractive children. He sat on the city council of Virginia City. A respected lawyer in his early forties, he seemed destined for higher office. Some said Mayor, or Governor, maybe even a United States Senator. Jefferson couldn't afford to let scandal interfere with his aspirations. He made only one mistake and Buela had found the man to make him pay for it.

Stryker walked out of the Silver Queen and went searching for the telegraph office.

"Yes, there's a couple foreigners who send telegrams kinda regular," the telegrapher told him. "Who's asking, mister."

Stryker left, realizing that he shouldn't have inquired so directly. At least he hadn't specified a Frenchman. Standing watch outside the office wouldn't do any good either, couldn't tell a man's nationality just by looking at him. For the time being, he'd let Buela do the asking. The next place he planned to visit was Piper's Opera House. He resolved to be less conspicuous about trying to locate Montel in the future. He headed for the assay office and Ivory, better to fade back into the role of bodyguard for now.

He found Ivory still in the assay office, carefully removing fragile pieces of equipment and labeled chemicals, some in large metal containers, others painstakingly packed in glass jars. He handled each item with a delicate proficiency normally ascribed to a medical doctor, certainly not a huge bull of a man more likely to destroy the china shop instead of arranging an artful display.

"Looks to be in good order," Ivory said, wiping his hands with a clean cloth. "I was afraid some of the stuff wouldn't get here in one piece. That woman give you all you need for your book?" Ivory asked, with a cynical grin.

"More than you know." Stryker picked up a jar and read the label. "When do you start what you came here for?"

"Tomorrow, right after breakfast." Ivory lay the cloth aside. "Careful with that cyanide. It's lethal. Not a good thing to spill."

"I know, saw a feller drink it."

"He drank it?" Ivory asked, eyebrows arching up his forehead.

"Pissed off a woman," Stryker deadpanned. "How much of this stuff you got?"

"Enough to test sample ore for a week, why?"

"Don't want you running low." Stryker sat the jar on the table. "I'm hungry."

"I know a place, Palace Saloon," Ivory suggested. He finished placing a jar filled with solvent back in its box. "Hey, wait!" Ivory grabbed his coat and hurried to catch up with Stryker who'd already gone out the door.

"God-damn Stryker," Ivory cursed, after coming up alongside of Stryker. "Do you even know where it is?"

"I know."

"Well hell, you coulda . . . Say, what the Sam Hell is your problem?"

"Didn't invite you to eat with me."

"We're supposed to be working together!"

"Working together is all."

"I'm coming anyway."

Stryker then realized Ivory was anxious about a black man eating by himself in the saloon. "Then you buy dinner."

If the streets in Virginia City weren't as crowded as normal, it was because everyone had gone inside the Palace Saloon. A banner, which read "World Arm Wrestling Championship" in bright yellow letters, hung on a rope stretched across the saloon, one roped end wrapped around the top of a mirror frame's finial behind the bar, and the other end tied to a brass hook screwed into the opposite wall.

"Let's go someplace else," Stryker shouted to Ivory upon seeing the throng of men and some women packed shoulder to shoulder inside. It almost seemed as if the tobacco smoke hanging in the air didn't have room to drift lower. The outgoing tide of men holding money above their heads, pushing toward the back, flowed against the incoming current straining to reach the bar. Neither wave seemed to be making any progress.

"Hey, mister!" Ivory grabbed a man by his upper arm, and pulled him closer. . "What's goin' on?"

The miner simply raised a hand and pointed at the banner.

"Yeah, I know that!"

"Outside!" The miner motioned for Ivory to follow him.

Stryker and Ivory trailed the man out the door.

"It's the world championship, right here in Virginia City," the miner boasted. "Last year they held it in Saint Louis or Chicago . . . some big city back East!"

"In a saloon?" Ivory asked, struggling mightily to hold back a smile, if not an outright laugh. "Men come from all over for it? Who brought it to Virginia City?" Ivory couldn't contain himself. He broke into a laugh before finishing the questions.

"Man named Millard owns the saloon." The minor squinted one eye shut. "Say mister, not much future for a man who makes fun of Outlaw Dave." The miner's excitement fell from his face.

"Who's Outlaw Dave?" Ivory asked.

"I am." And yeah, men do come from all over. The winner gets twenty-thousand."

Suddenly, the humor vanished from Ivory's face. "Twenty-thousand dollars? Where do they get that kind of money?"

"Yep, twenty-thousand dollars. This is Virginia City mister, millions come outta these hills." Excitement leapt back on the miner's face.

"Can I enter this thing?" Ivory asked, sounding incredulous.

"Better hurry. Competition starts in two hours."

"I'll eat at the Silver Queen," Stryker said, turning away. "You still pay."

Ivory watched Stryker's back briefly before shoving his way through the door and muscling his huge body through the crowd.

The steak he charged to Ivory was as good as any cut of meat Stryker had ever eaten. He'd finished all of it and was sipping his second beer when Buela joined him.

"There is a little Frenchman who makes regular visits to the telegraph office," she said. "I don't know where he sends 'em. I ask a few of the girls and one of them told me that much. This man doesn't pay us visits and all they, or she knows, is he goes there almost every day."

"How do you know he's French?" Stryker asked. He sipped his beer and returned the glass mug to the table. "Who's the woman? What you'd tell her?"

"She's a good friend. With me that night, actually, both times you know, both births. She knows what Franklin did, but she don't say nothing cause she's 'fraid what he might do. I told her I wanted to know if there's a Frenchman sending a lot of telegrams. Said to her, 'don't ask me any questions' and she ain't ask any. She probably figures I have my reasons. Like I said, she's a good friend." Buela watched Stryker lift the glass again. "You want to know her?"

"No."

"You haven't told me what you want with him. If he done somethin' bad, like Franklin, I hope you kill him too."

"Just get the man's name sending the telegrams." Stryker took a full minute to look around the saloon. "Does this Franklin fellow come in here for drinks?"

"Everybody comes in here. Why?" Buela glanced over Stryker's shoulder. "Here comes your friend."

"That last miner damn near broke my arm!" Ivory said, rubbing his elbow as he drew back a chair.

"No twenty-thousand," Stryker asked.

"Forty-five hundred." Ivory grumbled. "Got second. They split the money. Winner got ten. I forget what the rest of 'em got." He plopped in the chair to sulk. "I need something stronger than a beer," Ivory muttered, redirecting his attention to the bar. "Must've pulled somethin'." He tried straightening his arm but couldn't. "Ahh!" His face grimaced in pain.

"What do you want? I'll get it," Buela offered.

"Whiskey, the bottle." Ivory dropped his injured arm below the table and massaged his elbow. "Maybe it wasn't worth it. And we gotta go down that damn hole tomorrow. Shit."

"See a doctor first," Stryker said.

Ivory grimaced again and groaned, "I think you're right."

"Here." Buela sat the bottle and glass on the table. "Two dollars."

Ivory abandoned his injured arm and dug the money from his pocket. "You think a doctor would be around tonight?"

"Ezra Kleinman keeps a room over his office on B Street. You can probably find him . . . never mind. That's him over there, the man in the scruffy gray suit, white hair, and spectacles hanging on the end of his nose." Buela pointed toward a short plumpish man standing and talking with two other men at the bar's end.

Ivory poured the rye whiskey to the brim of the stout glass and emptied it in two long, face-contorted, gulps. Stryker couldn't tell if the contortions were caused by the elbow pain or the whiskey. He sipped from his own glass as he watched Ivory rise, his bad arm cradled in the other, and make his way across the saloon floor. The doctor shook his head angrily, evidently refusing to be interrupted from drinking and conversing with the two men. The refusal prompted Ivory to dig in his pocket and withdraw a wad of cash. Ivory waved it at the doctor and said something Stryker couldn't make out, but he suspected whatever Ivory told him, it was enough to change the good doctor's mind. Without taking leave given to his two friends, Doc Kleinman finished his drink in one long swallow and headed for the door with Ivory following closely behind him, dodging miners who might bump his arm.

"Let's go up to Piper's," Buela suggested. "Lily Langtry's come to town." Upon seeing Stryker's recalcitrant attitude, she added, "c'mon mister hard man, everybody will be there. Everybody, and you need to know what Franklin looks like." Buela's own expression turned dark.

"Let's go," Stryker said.

They climbed the stairs to the second floor of the Silver Queen and Buela led him down the long hallway to the rear door of the hotel. Because of the rise of elevation from the hotel's front they exited out the back on ground level, on B Street. Piper's Opera House sat on the corner of B Street and Union. A long train of raucous men, most carrying beer glasses had lined up in front of Piper's and down B Street. However another, shorter line, composed of nattily dressed men and women in stylish dresses, extended along B Street in the opposite direction. Stryker and Buela got in that line. Buela crooked her arm in one of Stryker's, and together they shuffled to the entrance where the ticket taker gave Buela a knowing nod. They climbed the wide stairway to the second floor and came to the main audience floor and the slanted stage. The floor, a large, level, wooden platform on springs, was John Piper's idea, who claimed it put a little spring into one's step. They took one more flight of stairs to the balcony level.

"Balcony, right side," the usher said, returning two ticket stubs to Buela.

An usher met them at the foot of the stairs and guided them to front row seats on the balcony. Good seats and discreet enough not to be seen by Virginia City's upper crust seated in the ground level front rows below. The next twenty minutes dragged by as the theater filled. Then, another long twenty minutes passed after the show was supposed to start. Miss Langtry obviously wanted her audience brought to near madness before she appeared. And, they were. The unruliest had downed the last drops of beer from their glasses and cocked their throwing arms when the curtains parted.

The audience grew suddenly quiet, enraptured by the famous actress's appearance. But, Lily wasn't on the stage. Other characters, some seated, some standing, began the vaudeville performance. A grumbling crescendo roiled the theater. Men, lifting themselves half out of their seats, craned their necks searching for the famous damsel. The play began on stage and had progressed but a few lines when the great actress appeared. The room erupted in a cacophony of whooping and clapping. Lily delivered her lines with exaggerated expressions and gestures, much to the delight of the enthralled. And then, she stepped to the front of the stage and belted out a French song only five men in the audience understood. She did this several more times; reverting to dramatic acting in a scene, followed by center stage solo musical performances, sometimes in French, some in English, always with great flair. Each vocal inflection or grand gesture evoked much swooning from the audience.

Buela smiled and applauded politely. Stryker didn't even do that much. He'd already figured a woman who was so full of herself, wouldn't be good in the sack. And, if she happened to get a good hard fucking, she would probably be possessive or petulant. He was glad when the performance was over.

Buela and Stryker left Piper's and took the same alley as before, heading back to the Silver Queen. Only one other couple made their way along the alley. They exited the opera house before Buela and Stryker had descended from balcony level and managed to worm their way through the crowd leaving by the front entrance. However, the couple strode leisurely arm in arm with the woman's head resting on the man's shoulder and was overtaken half-way. Buela, at first didn't recognize them in the darkness. Then, she did, the man anyway.

"Hello, Franklin."

Franklin and Jezebel, jolted from their romantic mood, pivoted around to search quizzically for the greeter's identity.

"I'm sorry, dear. Do we know you?" Jezebel directed the question at Buela, but it was the menacing man beside her who captured her attention. Jezebel pressed herself closer to Franklin.

"You probably don't know me Mrs. Jefferson, but your husband does."

Stryker inched away from Buela. This wasn't how he wanted, or expected, the confrontation would go with the Jefferson man. Killing a man in front of his wife, generally, wouldn't be a good idea. Not because of consideration for the woman. That didn't bother him so much. Rather, she would be a witness unless he shot her too. This is not a good time Buela, Stryker said to himself. Even if Jefferson doesn't try anything, there could still be a hell of a cat fight. He edged closer to Jefferson.

"You must be mistaken, Miss . . . whatever your name is. My husband wouldn't consort with someone like you," Jezebel spat. "Even in a dark alley, I can see you dress like a saloon woman."

"He knows me all right. I had his baby."

"What??? Jezebel looked incredulously at Buela, then at her husband. "Frank, what is she talking about? Do you have a child with this woman?"

"Not, anymore. He killed her." Buela glared at Franklin.

"I've had enough of this!" Franklin desperate to end the damaging revelations, groped for the small revolver he wore inside his suit jacket. But Stryker had already snaked a hand to the sai behind his back and with a blur of speed, smashed the center prong against Franklin's hand. The gun landed in the dirt.

"I know you drown my baby in the wash basin, Franklin. She was alive when you took her from me. And when you brought her back to my bed, my baby girl was dead.

"Frank! She's lying! Isn't she?" Jezebel saw Franklin's face and even in the shadows, she knew the truth. "You killed her baby?" She took her arm from his. A mask of horror crept onto her face. "Frank?"

"I had to. She'd have ruined us!" Jefferson's voice rose defensively.

"Now you're gonna pay," Buela said through gritted teeth.

Jezebel stooped and picked up the dropped revolver.

Stryker switched the sai to his left hand and pulled his own gun. He didn't bring it to bear on the woman, not just yet.

He didn't have to. Jezebel pointed the gun at her husband and fired three shots, cocking and firing the last two as he lay on the ground. She dropped the gun beside her dead husband. "You bastard."

Stryker took Buela's arm. "Let's go." They left Jezebel in the alley.

"You know, Stryker," Buela said, on the way back to the Silver Queen, "I don't blame her." When Stryker didn't respond, evidently figuring it best not to comment, she added, "not because he cheated on her, nor even for killing my baby, but because he had a child with another woman."

Stryker wisely chose not to question the woman's reasoning.

Jezebel recounted the incident accurately to the sheriff. The shocked lawman said to the equally stunned councilmen that he believed the woman. The hastily called council meeting lasted two hours, after which they asked the new widow to join them. They explained to her, Franklin would have hanged for what he did. They thanked her for apprehending a murderer, and that they could see she had no choice but to shoot a man resisting arrest. They also expressed deep concern for her children. So, they said, all things being considered, rather than perpetuating an embarrassment to the city council and especially to Mrs. Jefferson, they thought it best to slightly alter the shape of events. The *Territorial Enterprise* headline read "COUNCILMAN FRANKLIN JEFFERSON GUNNED DOWN IN BRUTAL ROBBERY." Jezebel's name was not mentioned.

The following morning Ivory, sporting a new white arm sling, joined Stryker downstairs. Stryker was bent over his usual steak and eggs.

"Elbow was out of joint," Ivory said, scraping back a chair. "He couldn't pull it so he tied his belt onto my wrist and a doorknob. Little bastard surprised me and shoved me hard in the damn chest. Knocked me on my heels, and it popped in. Still sore," Ivory said, rubbing the white cloth over his elbow. Then, on the way back, I got fuckin' robbed. I guess waving that cash around wasn't so smart but I had to get my arm fixed. Shit. There were four of 'em, two shotguns. Dark in the alley, couldn't get a good look at 'em. All I got outta last night is a banged-up elbow. Don't that beat all."

"Overcooked the eggs," Stryker said. He shoved them to the edge of his plate and attacked the steak.

"You're the bodyguard. The deal remember?" Ivory rubbed his arm as he spoke.

"Can't protect you from your own stupidity." Stryker alluded to Ivory flashing cash the night before. "Do what you came for."

"I guess I shouldn't have arm wrestled alright. But that damn doc wasn't gonna fix me. I had to show him the money!" Seeing Stryker wasn't moved, Ivory gave up explaining. "We go down the Combination this morning, thirty-three hundred feet down into the bowels of earth. It gets hot down there, real hot."

'I find the Frenchie, I'm gone," Stryker growled.

"You don't have him yet. Wagon's waiting."

Stryker snatched his hat off the table and grabbed the Winchester leaning against his chair. They walked out of the Silver Queen to a Columbus freight wagon, loaded, and waiting in front with a four horse team.

"I got everything on this here list, Mister Ivory," the wagon driver called Gimp, said. "The assay office man filled the order and he marked off every item." When he jumped from the wagon, Stryker recognized him as the same man who'd stabled the roan, the cripple.

Gimp drove the buckboard south through town. As they rode away from the clamor of Virginia City, the constant drumming of 200 mills Stryker had been hearing but not paying attention to, became louder. When Ivory noticed him searching for the source, "stampers crushing ore," he said. They turned eastward at the south end of Six Mile Canyon and then back north along a hill peppered with pinion pines. Ivory pointed to the mill a quarter mile away. "That's it." As they rolled closer, Stryker saw "Combination Mine" in large letters emboldened on the building's side.

"They've dug a shaft down nearly thirty-three hundred feet, three a day," Ivory said. "It's a hundred and thirty degrees down there and they pump five million gallons of hot, steamin' water a day out that hole. After we have a look, I'm most likely gonna shut it down and there'll be a lot of unhappy men. They've been makin' four dollars a day. That's why you're here Stryker."

"Shoulda brought a shotgun," Stryker growled.

"Inside the shaft building, a steam driven hoist engine winches cables over the sheave wheels, at least eight feet high. It'll raise and lower the cage we'll be on. You can really hear the stampers now. Inside it's deafening." Ivory had begun to talk louder over the ore crushing machine which, even outside the building's walls, pounded a person's innards. He pointed at the huge mounds of tailings downhill from the mine. "That's ore they've already processed. All wasted, hardly any silver in it. Let's go inside." Ivory jumped from the wagon and went around and dropped the tailgate. "Gimp, help me with these scales." Ivory ordinarily could hoist the four-foot scales to his shoulder and carry them by himself, but his elbow still bothered him. Stryker trailed behind the two men carrying the heavy weighing instrument to the backdoor of the building. The road and rail tracks led up to that entrance, although they entered at ground level, it was actually the second floor up from the lower downhill level. Having higher and wider than normal-sized doors, it could accommodate larger pieces of equipment. Ivory and Gimp sat the scales on a work bench.

"Stryker, come with me. Let's go find the supervisor," Ivory yelled, looking around the mill. Ivory and Stryker made their way across the floor, walking past the horizontal steam hoist, a beast at rest, releasing occasional bursts of steam, and along a rail where below, they saw the stampers, also steam driven, crushing melon-sized rocks. The incessant thumping vibrated the entire body. The place smelled of heavy oil and grease, and rock dust coated their noses and throats. However, the loud noise smothered everything else in the brain, and miners quickly learned to read lips.

Closing the door to the supervisor's office behind Ivory and Stryker did little to dull the din outside. A stout man of average height turned from the window when the shaft house clamor had rushed through the open door. A scowl spread over his ruddy face, signaling his annoyance at being interrupted, and at being assaulted with the mining racket that had been somewhat mitigated from inside the office.

"You here to close us down?" And seeing Stryker following with the Winchester canted on his shoulder, Tucker asked, "Who's he?"

"Going down the shaft to have a look and I want to see ore samples. Then decide." Ivory hooked a thumb at Stryker beside him. "He's here to help with the deciding."

Tucker glared at the big man for several long seconds before he spoke. "We're waitin' on black powder from town. Ain't no diggin' right now, but we can run you down now if you want. You'll need lamps and ice."

"I'll get a pick and shovel, and a couple more things." Ivory said. "Meet you at the lift. You coming down?"

"Gotta pay for the powder when they get here. I'll be at the cage in ten minutes with the lights and ice, and I'll wait for you up top. You remember the bells?"

"One for hoist to stop and go, two for lower, nine for danger." Ivory replied.

Tucker nodded.

"Let's go Stryker," Ivory said, turning for the door.

They left the supervisor's office and headed back to the wagon outside. Ivory dug out a pick, shovel, short-handled pick, long and short jack hammers, and spikes of various sizes, bucket, and brushes. He put the spikes and brushes in the bucket. "Won't you give Gimp your Winchester, and help me carry this stuff, Stryker. Just you and me in that hole, I guess."

"You carry the shit, Gimp." Stryker ordered. He dropped the carbine off his shoulder and caught its barrel in his left hand.

They carried the equipment to the lift cage where Tucker waited with two Davy safety lamps. Tucker lit them and handed each to Ivory and Stryker. Ivory stepped inside the cage and inspected the ice crates placed on the lift.

Gimp dumped his load in the cage and Stryker handed the Winchester to him. "Make good use of this if you have to." That said, the mixed-breed turned to Tucker. "Get a lamp for yourself."

"I'm not going down."

Stryker drew the Peacemaker in one smooth motion. "Get it." He thumbed the hammer, cocking the Colt. "You better hope your men love their boss."

Stryker followed the supervisor to a cabinet propped against a wall just beyond the lift. A wooden cabinet, six feet high and just as wide, it had screened doors so that you could see the mining lamps stacked on the shelves inside. Stryker thought Tucker fumbled a bit too much with the latch.

After all the tools were in the lift, Tucker and Stryker stepped on.

"Bring her down!" The supervisor leaned out over the waist high cage gate and signaled the hoist engineer, a bearded fellow wearing suspenders and standing by the gear handles of the massive steam engine. The drum spool winder began playing out cable and the lift started down with a jolt. Stryker and Ivory grabbed the sides of the cage to balance themselves. The creaking of the cage became more noticeable as it dropped away from the clamor above. When Stryker looked up at the rectangular light at the top, he could see it growing smaller and smaller. Besides the cage groans, an occasional rattle of the pipe carrying scalding hot water from the bottom of the mine was the only other sound to be heard in the shaft.

"Ivory, if this mine fails, Virginia City is finished." Tucker shined his light on Ivory's face as he spoke. "We have to go this deep to find another pay zone of silver. Everything above is played out. This is our last hope. You can't shut us down."

"Losing money on a mine won't keep the town goin,' " Ivory replied. "Besides, workin' men down in this hellhole is inhuman. Damn, it's getting hot."

Tucker took his light off Ivory and put it on the gate. The lift began to slow. When it came to a full stop Tucker flipped the latch and stepped out onto the bottom of the mine, covered with two inches of water. Ivory and Stryker followed.

"Show me your last dig, Tuck." Ivory said, splashing ahead of the supervisor, throwing his lamp light around the jagged rock walls. "You pull anything worthwhile outta here?"

"No."

Ivory used the short-handled pick to jab at the rock. His digging was more for show than for any useful purpose. "When's the last time you mined good ore? Damn, it's hot."

"We never have."

Tucker heard it first. Rather, he was the first to realize he didn't hear it. "The pumps have stopped." He ran through water now four inches deep and ran the bell nine times. "Get on! We gotta go up!"

Ivory and Stryker scrambled onto the lift.

"Ring it again!" Ivory yelled.

Tucker rang again, and then three more times, each a series of nine bell rings. "Shit. They're gonna flood it." He swung outside the cage, propped a boot on the upper edge of the opened gate, and hoisted himself on the steel mesh top.

Ivory climbed on top next with help from Tucker who pulled, and Stryker who pushed.

"Reckon it'll look more like an accident if you die too." Stryker directed his light at the supervisor. "How much time?"

"Only a few minutes. Even if you could climb the loose rock, which you can't, the water will rise twenty-feet an hour. And the cable's greased."

"We'll scald to death." Ivory added. "This is what you planned for me and Stryker, you son of a bitch!" He attempted to cock his right arm but the sling got in the way, and he delivered a powerful jab with his left instead. Even if the blow wasn't with its intended force, it still knocked Tucker against the rock, and he had to push back mightily to keep from falling between the wall and cage.

"I don't want to die in this fucking hole," Ivory yelled. "Think of something! Ring the fucking bell again!"

"Keep ringing it until I tell you to stop," Stryker ordered.

Thirty minutes later, the water had reached the top of the cage and was creeping up the boots of the three men.

"Stryker, your gun," Tucker said.

"I always thought I'd die in the arms of a pretty girl. She wouldn't have to love or even know me. Just be impressed with my bravery," Ivory said, exhaling the last words with great resignation. Stryker, it's starting to poor down my boots!" He struggled to stand on his tiptoes. "Don't let me die like this!"

"Ivory, grab the ladder on the wall behind you," Stryker shouted.

"What? Where?" Ivory shined his lamp on the wall. "I don't see ..."

The shot reverberated within the walls of the mine shaft as the bullet smashed into the back of Ivory's head just beneath his cap.

Stryker turned the Peacemaker on Tucker.

"Make it quick," Tucker said.

Stryker did. "You can stop ringing the bell." He said, after Tucker's body collapsed into the water. Stryker looped Tucker's belt around the dead man's neck, dragged the body on top of Ivory's, and stood on it. He held the cable for balance, and waited.

At the top of the mine shaft, four men waited as well. Three of them miners, with one holding a Winchester pointed at the fourth, Gimp, who sat cross-legged on the floor.

A third shot rumbled up from the shaft. "That's three of 'em. Start the lift. Start the pump," said the miner holding the carbine. "Don't look at me like that. We had to do it," he groused. "The pump failed. A horrible accident. That's what happened. And Gimp, you keep your mouth shut. Won't just be you who'll get shot. Your wife and kids too. Better, you should leave town."

As the cable started to wind out of the black void below, the four men stood anxiously at the mouth of the mine shaft. Then, when they heard the creaking cage nearing the top, all but the gun holder eased themselves back from the hole, perhaps a subconscious move by the three, not wanting to view the aftermath of what happened below.

"Here it comes," the miner with the gun said. He gripped barrel tighter. Upon seeing three bodies massed on top of the cage, he announced, "they're all dead."

The sight of the futile effort to survive may have caused the gunman to miss a small movement--the barrel of Stryker's resting .44 protruding between Tucker's arm and torso, swiveled slightly before belching fire and lead. The slug flattened as it smacked into the man's chest, driving him off his feet. Stryker lunged and grabbed the Winchester off the floor with his left hand, and with his right fired two more rounds with the Colt.

Before Stryker could bring the carbine to bear on Gimp, he cried out, "They jumped me from behind!"

"He's right!" yelled the hoist machinist, who had remained by the gears. The pump operator came forward and chimed, "They said they'd kill us, and our wives." He lowered his voice as his words slowed to a crawl.

"You!" Stryker pointed the barrel at the lift operator. 'The dynamite, where is it?"

"That crate. Caps there too." He volunteered the location of the blasting caps.

"You know how to set it?"

"I guess so."

"Place half-dozen sticks in the hoist gears and another six under the pump. Light the fuses when you got 'em set," Stryker shouted to the lift operator. He then he called to the pump operator. "Kill it!"

"What about the rest of the miners?" The machinist asked as he dug out the dynamite and caps.

"Gimp!" Stryker yelled. He swung the gun barrel at the pump operator and fired. "Leave."

Stryker followed the machinist to the hoist. "You gonna shoot me too?"

"Set 'em right or go down the hole."

When the dynamite was set and fuses lit, Stryker shot him.

The small army of men was three hundred yards down the hill when the mine blew.

CHAPTER EIGHT

The townsfolk had poured out on the streets of Virginia City and several of the men rushed to meet the wagon rolling a quarter mile ahead of the miners.

"What happened?" The fastest of the group, yelled.

Gimp waited until the rest of the men caught up. "The mine inspector and Tucker died in the shaft. Others died in the blast. The mine's shut down."

They rode on past the crowd, who stood staring at the remains of the Combination Mine on the hill. Gimp stopped the wagon in front of the Silver Queen where Stryker hopped off. He offered a quick nod to the mixed-breed and snapped the reins.

"I heard an explosion," Buela said. She handed Stryker a beer as he crossed the doorway. "Where's your big black friend?"

"Dead."

"Let's sit."

They sat at table, Stryker nursing his beer, Buela sipping tea, neither talking.

The saloon was nearly empty since only three hard drinkers had come in off the street. The remaining patrons rushed outside and stood staring at the hill on the far side of the valley. Smoldering rubble of the mine's buildings, that's all that was left of it. Mesmerized, the scattered groups of people talked in hushed voices with each other.

Presently, Gimp came inside. When he entered the almost deserted saloon, he looked around awkwardly, surprised by finding only five people in it. Three men sat alone at different tables drinking. Stryker and Buela sat on the far side of the saloon. He crossed the floor to their table.

"Beer?" Buela asked.

"Reckon I could use something a little stronger."

"Whiskey." Buela raised her arm and motioned to the bartender.

"Leave the bottle," Stryker ordered, when the bartender filled Gimp's glass.

"What happened up there?" Buela ventured.

"Ask him." Stryker pushed back and got up from the table. He gripped the whiskey bottle at the neck and lifted his glass. "Buela, send a girl to my room." He made a half turn. "A pretty one. Two of 'em."

"Okay, Gimp, what the hell went on up there?" Buela watched Stryker walk up the stairs.

"Him and Ivory went down the shaft. Stryker made Tucker go with 'em. You know Tucker, I guess. He runs the mine. He's the supervisor. Been there since they . . ."

"Christ sakes! Get on with it!" Buela's patience with Gimp had thinned.

"Tucker and them planned to flood the shaft while Stryker and Ivory wuz in it."

"Damn them." Buela interrupted.

"The bastards did it anyway, even with Tucker down there." Gimp took a gulp of the whiskey. "One of 'em grabbed me from behind. Made me sit on the floor while they did it. Took the rifle Stryker had gave me 'fore they went down. He must've knowed somethun'. Then, after a while, when we knowed they surely wuz in a bad way, we heard three shots. Figured they chose to kill themselves so as not to scald to death. Reckon Stryker shot Ivory and Tucker."

"So that's it. He killed Ivory." Buela reasoned. And, he shot Tucker. Maybe he didn't matter, but that's two men he killed today."

"Two hell! He killed half of 'em in the God-damned mine! Kilt three of 'em quicker'n a fly fart. Then he shot two more. Just walked over and shot 'em. Didn't never blink. That man is one hard son of a bitch, Miss Buela. Got cold evil eyes."

A hint of a smile crept its way onto Buela's lips.

"Jesus, Miss Buela, why you grinning? You like that? God, what is it with you women? Likin' a killer like him?"

"Leader of the pack, Gimp." Buela allowed a short laugh. "Leader of the pack. I better go get the girls." She started to rise.

"So what's he want them girls for?"

"I imagine he'll fuck 'em."

"Well, you didn't have to . . ." Gimp tried to look embarrassed. "I knowed that," he said, gazing absently toward the stairway. "Figured he ain't remorseful. But, if he's grieving, he sure knows how to grieve."

Twenty-six hours later, Buela came through the doors of the Silver Queen to find Stryker eating steak, eggs, and a pile of pancakes. He glanced her way as she approached.

"Worked up an appetite, didn't you." Buela said.

"It's been a day and a half."

"Bragging?"

"Since I ate."

She took in the effects of his freshly scrubbed appearance, clean shirt, and slicked back hair. His morning shave stopped short of scraping off *all* the whiskers. "Looks like you got a bath. They clean you up too?"

Stryker cut off a piece of steak and stabbed it with his fork. "They fussed over me 'til I got in the tub, twice actually. One yesterday, one today."

"They said you paid well."

"They earned it." Stryker gulped a swallow of black coffee and cut into the steak. "Why'd you come over here?"

"Got news on your Frenchman."

Stryker rested his forearms, clutching knife and fork in hand on the table. "What's the news?"

"He was here all right."

"Was."

"Was, sorry to say. One of the girls let it slip; a man from San Francisco was looking for him. He caught a train night before last, headed to Utah."

"Couldn't tell me earlier?"

"Just found out, myself, Stryker. As they say in France, shit."

"Shit."

"Sometimes you get the gold, sometimes you get your man, and sometimes . . . you get the shaft."

"Reckon so." Stryker said, acknowledging irrefutable logic.

"I did find out he bought a ticket to Ogden. Sure you don't want to stay here for a while longer?" Buela asked, with a puckish smile.

"I've wasted enough time, Buela. I need to find the bastard. Have him sign what he's supposed to sign, and get back to California."

"Oh, I thought you wanted to kill him." Buela said, sounding surprised. "If I had known all you wanted was for him to sign something, I'd've had one of my girls get his mark. Dammit. Want one on the house before you go? I feel kinda bad."

"No." Stryker pushed back from the table, leaving most of his breakfast on the plates. "Besides, I'm about out of bullets."

The next train to Salt Lake was scheduled for the following day. Stryker left the train depot cursing himself over straying from his intended mission, for a number of reasons, primarily among them, was the woman in San Francisco. Dammit Morgan, if you want a saint, you should marry one. Besides, the last man who was perfect got nailed to a cross for his virtue. Nevertheless, he reprimanded himself, and decided in the future, to let his brain do the thinking, and not that "fellow" below the waist.

Oddly, he felt a spark of remorse for having shot Ivory. He kind of wished he'd thought of firing the third shot sooner. But he hadn't. It only occurred to him after he bought a few more minutes standing on the two men's bodies.

However, killing the big black man had nothing to do with the two girls at the hotel. The real reason was a nagging notion lying in the weeds of his mind. That woman in San Francisco might not want him taking off on long rides alone. What if she angled persuasively for him to grow roots in the city? Start a business he'd have to run. Wear different clothes. Sell the roan. And she surely wouldn't be gleeful if he got a couple of prostitutes every now and then, for God's sake.

He guessed those girls represented a rebellion of sorts. Yeah, almost as if he could feel the ropes starting to tighten and he threw 'em off. Nevertheless, a good woman is hard to come by. And, this one was special in more ways than one. A corner of his mouth twitched. He remembered an old timer's advice. "You can pull a freight train with a woman's quim whisker."

Stryker stopped at the telegraph office and sent a message to Hearst, informing him about Ivory, the mine, and Montel's leaving for Utah. Of course, the telegram had to be too brief to mention many particulars. He also got the roan ready, inspecting the animal, and packing what he needed in the saddle bags. That night he read the *Examiner* in his room.

It seemed as if he was spending most of his life on trains, especially the last few months. Maybe it saved time and a sore body. However, Stryker began to itch for a ride, a long solitary ride, on a horse. He was also starting to question his chasing this damn Frenchie all over the place. Stryker, never a man to quit, nevertheless had to admit to himself something about this quest didn't feel right. He couldn't figure it out, but the incessant gnawing in his gut wouldn't go away. In fact, he found it getting bigger and impossible to ignore. He should have gotten his man, but chiding himself can't help. Find the bastard. Make him sign the God-Damned Deed. That's what's important. He owed it to Hearst. Not catching the Frenchman in Virginia City was his fault. Now he had to rectify it.

"A ticket to Ogden," Stryker said to the ticket master the next morning. He started to turn away from the window and stopped. "You sold a ticket to a French fellow a couple of days ago. You remember what he looked like?"

"Yeah, I reckon." The clerk eyed Stryker suspiciously. He evidently decided it wiser to anger the departed Frenchman than the fearsome figure of a man in front of him. "About my height, short like me, I guess." He raised his hand level with his head. "He had short brown hair, tan, and kind of a sissified devil, if you ask me. Anything else, mister?"

"How many stops between here and Ogden?"

The terrain flattened out east of Reno. Expansive level ground had sagebrush, bitterbrush, and other shrubs clinging to life on the high desert. A few juniper and pinion pines poked out of the ground on occasion. Rocky hills cropped up in the distance, mountains loomed farther out. The rigors of the past two days left Stryker pretty tired. He actually saw little of the landscape. He slept most of the trip.

Stryker inquired at each stop about the Frenchman. No station attendants remembered a man looking or talking like Montel exiting the train. It wasn't until the next morning in Ogden, after traveling sixteen hours on the train that Stryker finally spoke to someone who saw a man fitting Montel's description. The helpful Mormon said he thought the Frenchman met up with four Conestoga wagons heading south to Salt Lake and he didn't know where from there. He added the folks on the wagons were no longer welcome in Ogden, nor in Salt Lake he guessed, since those people had broken away from The Latter Day Saints teachings, calling themselves "Fundamentalists." That had been two days ago.

The Mormon tugged on his beard. "There's another wagon fixin' to leave to catch up with 'em. They might could use a rider goin' along. There's only the four of them. Even though we don't agree wit' 'em no more, wouldn't want to see 'em scalped. No pay, they don't have much money."

"Where do I find them?"

"Johnson's Livery. Gettin' the wagon repaired. That's why they're behind the other four."

Stryker tipped the brow of the Stetson.

Leading the roan south along 25th street, the Western edge of the Wasatch Mountains loomed off to Stryker's left, and he could see patches of snow still hanging on the highest peaks. Passing several of the town's citizenry, Stryker wondered if the uniform of the day for women was long dresses and bonnets. They all looked the same. The livery and stable came into view after he'd gone about two hundred paces down the street. He hadn't seen it earlier since it sat back a ways from the other buildings, isolated, with livestock corrals on both sides of the shop. As he passed a feed and tack store and stopped at the livery, the smell of animal waste hit his nostrils.

Stryker found the man and three women seated outside Johnson's Blacksmith and Livery. The man wore a long black woolen coat, a gray shirt underneath, buttoned up to the sweat-stained collar. The women wore long-sleeved, ankle-length, non-frivolous dresses which had vestiges of a long past heavy starch. The back end of a wagon jutted out from the livery. An ox team stood in one of the adjacent corrals. Inside, a heavy hammer banged on metal.

"I'll be riding with you until you catch up with the other wagons." Startled, the man looked up to see a not too friendly looking Stryker, a big roan horse standing behind him. Suddenly a huge explosive smile replaced the initial surprised countenance. "God be praised!" He leapt to his feet, the three women following obediently. "Our Heavenly Father has provided protection on our journey to Canaan." Turning to the women, "Praise be unto him." They smiled, looking somewhat relieved. Turning back to Stryker, he extended his hand. Stryker rejected it and Jacob swept it toward the women to save face. "I'm called Jacob, and my wives," pointing to the women with an open palm, "Rebecca, Mabel, and Alacrity." The three nodded, briefly dipping their bonnets.

Jacob, a spry, handsome man who looked to be in his early thirties at the most, had a closely cropped beard, blue eyes, and blond hair which hung down to his shoulders. All three of the women, peering out from their bonnets, wore plain dresses, but were easy on the eyes, especially Alacrity. A devout group to be sure, Stryker noted.

"How long 'til you're ready?" Stryker asked.

"Another half day I'm told." Jacob struggled to maintain the grin.

The smell of livestock gave way to the heavy odor of the forge and burnt metal as Stryker entered the blacksmith shop.

Stryker found the blacksmith heating a wheel axle in the forge. The wagon in the doorway blocked much of the outside sunlight and glowing embers from the forge cast the ironsmith's shadow on the opposite wall. The blacksmith, using tongs, pulled the red hot metal from the coke fire and placed it on an anvil's horn. He pounded the hammer with the muscular arms of a man who'd spent years working in the smithy, turning the axle after each blow.

"What you want?" The blacksmith grunted. He didn't look up from his work.

"How long for this?"

"Told you before. You not hear . . . ?" A glance at the mixed-breed cut him short. "Who are you?"

"Answer me."

"The burly blacksmith returned to his work. "Two axles, two hubs, two steel tires, and changing the trees from mules to oxen. Ain't going nowhere today."

Satisfied, Stryker turned and walked out of the livery. "Back later," he said to the four outside. He pulled the saddlebags from the roan and found a supply store to buy salt, beans, cured ham, potatoes, coffee, and a sack of oats for the roan. Then he stopped for a late breakfast and picked up a newspaper before returning to the livery.

"Jacob, you heading out tonight or in the morning?" Stryker asked.

"When the repairs are done sir. Our Lord will be our guiding light." Jacob sat on a barrel beside the three women resting on barrels as well. He kicked a small stone with the toe of his boot.

Stryker, still admonishing himself over letting Montel slip away in Virginia City, slipped the saddle off the roan and sat on it to read the paper. He'd read the paper from front to back, and dozed off twice before the blacksmith came out and announced the wagon was ready. He threw the saddle on the roan as Jacob led two oxen into the livery and yoked them to the wagon.

Jacob backed the Conestoga out and yoked up the remaining two teams for a total of six oxen on the wagon. He saw Stryker watching and said, "We switched from mules. Easier to handle and Indians steal horses and mules." He eyed the roan and added, "Slower though."

"Indian trouble?"

"Over the years here in Utah, we've had a history of depredations by the Utes and Paiutes. Lately, they've been less troublesome, but precautions are still necessary."

Stryker rode alongside the Conestoga, gathering more than his share of furtive, quizzical glances, as they made their way south out of Ogden. He guessed he hardly looked the part of a devout brother. Jacob sat between Rebecca and Mabel on the Conestoga's front bench. Alacrity rode inside.

CHAPTER NINE

"Thank you for joining me for dinner, Miss Bickford." Hearst rose and waited until the Maître D' seated Morgan before he settled back in his chair. He often dined in the private confines of the Tapestry Room at the Palace. That was especially true tonight since he did not wish his talk with Morgan to be overheard. "I woulda came up to the city sooner like you did but I stopped in San Simeon to camp with William. We like to spend what time we can there, you know. In fact, he told me, someday he wants to build a little something on the hill. Did you like Cayucos?" Before Morgan could answer he added, "John Cass likes Cayucos better than San Simeon. Not me."

"I've only seen San Simeon from a ship. I must visit there sometime. The hills look friendly." Morgan spread the napkin on her lap. "The visit with your friend in Cayucos was pleasant. I liked the pier."

A waiter interrupted, placing menus on the table and asking for drink preferences.

When alone again, Hearst launched into his real reason for asking Morgan to dinner. "Stryker weren't able to pin down Montel in Virginia City. I guess the rascal flew the coup, headed toward Utah." He noticed a hint of disappointment briefly crossed Morgan's face. "I wouldn't be asking our man to pursue him but William really wants to run the paper and that's the first time he's showed a interest in anything at all. And Morgan, that Montel had me believe I already *owned* the darn paper. He deceived me. He ain't getting away with that."

"Mr. Hearst, Stryker will find him. Montel will sign the paper over to you, but I'm not sure that man will survive their meeting."

"Ha, ha, I might think you're serious." Hearst laughed, as the waiter placed a glass of wine for Morgan and whiskey for Hearst, on the linen covered table.

"I am serious."

Hearst set the glass on the table without taking the intended drink. "He shouldn't a cheated me."

"No."

"Would you care to order ma'am, sir?" The waiter interrupted, obviously vying for a quick table turn over big a big tip.

Once they'd given their orders and the waiter had left them, Hearst revived their discussion. "I ain't a vindictive man. Otherwise, I'd have that young waiter cleaning toilets."

Morgan smiled and sipped a very good wine. "For a whiskey man, you chose a delightful grape."

"Does Stryker drink wine?" Hearst teased.

She treated the Senator to a quick and easy laugh. "No, whiskey and beer, or coffee."

"My near seventy years of living have taught me to know when a woman favors a man. Curious though."

"Why him?' Morgan asked. "I guess you're curious about Stryker."

"Yes."

"There are other reasons, of course, and I'll keep most of them to myself, but I'll mention a couple for you . . . he rings of good steel, I can't control him. And . . ." Morgan paused.

"And?"

"And he's killed for me."

"Jesus, Morgan!" Hearst sputtered, swallowing a mouthful of whiskey in one gulp. "Miss Bickford!"

Morgan glared intently at Hearst, as if daring disproval.

Hearst hesitated, then quickly recaptured his wits. "You two are sure right for one another." He smiled and said, "Want more wine?"

"Thank you, yes. After dinner, I would like you to meet a young couple from the theater. I've asked them to the hotel at eight o'clock," Morgan said.

The waiter returned shortly with a medium rare steak for the Senator and veal for Morgan. The rest of their conversation, interspersed throughout the enjoyment of a well-prepared meal, dwelt with such superfluous topics as San Francisco weather, growth of the city, and the arts. Mining and politics were held in abeyance so they could relish the excellent meal. Morgan's suggestion of a meeting afterwards with two people from the theater would seem to extend a fine evening. The dinner finished, the Senator smoked a cigar and Morgan took the last delicate sip of her second glass of wine.

"This couple, Miss Bickford, it ain't my habit to be a benefactor. I enjoy the theater like anyone. However, my support ends with the purchase of a ticket, or tickets. I bought season tickets. Lately though, I don't enjoy the performances as much."

"They're not here for your support, financial support, that is," Morgan replied. "I asked them here for another reason. They were reluctant to come. I promised them privacy. They don't want to be seen talking to you–us."

Hearst arched his eyebrows.

"You'll find out why," Morgan said.

"Where are they?"

"Outside, at a restaurant across the street, if they're still there."

"Bring them to my room here at the hotel." Hearst got to his feet and went around the table to scoot out Morgan's chair. "I'll wait for all of you up there."

A light drizzle greeted Morgan as she stepped outside and she drew the collar of her jacket tight around her neck. San Francisco wrapped its chill-you-to-the-bone arms around her and she shivered in its dampness. Wet cobblestones and cable rails glistened with reflections of street lamps and lights from stores and shops across Market Street. Horse drawn buggies passed by the animals' hooves loudly clopping on the wet stones. She waited for two cable cars to pass and then hurried across the street, careful not to trip on the slippery rails.

The couple from the theater acted reluctant to meet. They might have left the café. Then she saw them through the glass but didn't wave. Stan and Myrna, who were seated by a window in the Café Paree, watched Morgan walk out of the Palace toward them. Stan placed a hand on Myrna's and offered his wife a stilted smile, but she couldn't seem to muster the effort to return it. They refocused their attention on the woman crossing the street.

Morgan entered the café and went straight to the counter. She bought a coffee and brought it to the young couple's table. "I chose not to tell him what this is about. I'll give a brief background of the theater and we'll see where it goes from there. If you feel like taking over, go ahead. He'll probably ask questions. And, don't be too shy. Mister Hearst is a self-made man. Just because he's a Senator doesn't mean he's full of himself like a lot of politicians."

Stan, a tall angular man and Myrna, a pretty, petite girl, nervously gave each other looks that seem to ask should we do this.

Morgan saw and understood. "The audience, the public, doesn't know what's going on. Much is at stake and you can't do it by yourselves."

"Let's go." Stan stood and extended a hand to Myrna.

A tea pot and three cups sat on the round table moved to the room's center; placed there to welcome the Senator's guests into his suite. He rose when they entered and pointed an opened palm. "Hot tea for you on a cold night."

The couple hesitated and Morgan stepped forward to pour the tea. She gave cups to each and poured one for herself. She noticed Hearst had a half-filled glass of whiskey on his desk.

"Won't you be seated." Hearst pulled his desk chair around in front of the desk and picked up his whiskey, motioning toward a settee near him.

Morgan positioned a chair next to the couple.

"This is Stan and Myrna," Morgan began. They are both actors at the Savoy Theatre. Have you been there, George?" She used the Senator's first name to demonstrate how well she knew him, telling Stan and Myrna she could protect them.

"Not lately." Hearst sipped from his glass and smiled at Morgan, letting her know he liked her calling him George.

Morgan began. "There's a performance called *Worker Nation* playing now. It's about a man and wife, played by Stan and Myrna, who suffer horribly under labor conditions in the employment of a corporation. In this case, the company is called Toiler Industries, clever name." She paused to try her tea. "Eventually, the government intercedes, shuts down Toiler, and takes over. Working conditions dramatically improve, and our couple here, goes on to live happy and comfortable lives. Nice story isn't it? Only, it doesn't work that way. It was tried in Bickford, the town my husband and I built. A gang of men arrived and murdered him. They changed the town's name to Egalitaria. Everyone would be equal; all paid the same; regardless of their work. Eventually, people realized, why work? The most productive became like everybody else working at the lowest level, or not at all. To make matters worse, the gang who took over the town kept most of the money for themselves. We damn near starved."

"You never told me that Morgan," Hearst said. He turned and set his glass on the desk.

"Senator Hearst . . ." Stan began.

"Mister Hearst," the Senator corrected. "No need to be formal here."

"Something similar has happened at the Savoy. Before Barry Blankton and his wife bought the theater, we performed . . . just regular plays." Stan lifted his arms and spread his palms for emphasis. "Now, all we do is this stuff. And, we're told to say how wonderful working for the government would be, not only in the theater but outside it as well."

"Why you gonna along with it?" Hearst asked.

"Mister Hearst, actors are not discovered, or made. They're selected. There are hundreds of actors ready and willing to fill our shoes. That's one reason we don't make much money."

"You said one reason." Hearst invited more.

"The Blanktons have put the theaters into a charity. We're told we shouldn't expect higher pay, since it's a charity. But, they sure pay themselves well enough, living on Nob Hill. Anyway, if we don't do what they say, we'll be fired. And they're taking over more and more theaters. We couldn't find work if we're let go."

"Look, Mister Hearst," Myrna joined in, "We don't know anything about politics. We're actors. All we want to do is act. It wasn't until Miss Morgan confronted us outside the theater, that we realized something was wrong."

"We suspected it, actually, but kept quiet," Stan added.

"You see, George," Morgan said. "These agitators don't have to convince each performer, or each person on the street, one by one, the so-called miracle of a government run society. They gain control of theaters, or of newspapers, and trumpet this nonsense to the masses."

At the word, newspaper, Hearst straightened and scowled.

"And that is why Montel is clinging so hard to the *Examiner*," Morgan continued. "He's one of them. And that is why you must not call off getting it signed over to you. You have your own reasons as you've stated before, but this is far more important."

"I'll ask for a Senatorial committee to investigate them theaters. However, Morgan, as you know, the newspaper and theater might be a little tricky for me, First Amendment issue, and all."

"All the newspapers all give rave reviews to *Worker Nation*, I mean." Stan explained. "They sure support the Blankton's plays."

"Who the hell are them Blanktons? Where do they come from?" Hearst demanded.

"We don't really know sir. They just showed up. The Mitchells, who used to own the theaters, said they had no choice but to sell out, pretty cheap too," Stan said.

"A charity . . . seems odd. They wouldn't have to have a charity to pay low wages. Why go to the trouble?" Hearst asked.

"It's worse than all of you know, including you, Stan," Myrna broke in. "I work in the office too. I only have small parts in the plays. Stan is the main actor. Here's what I know. The Blanktons have influence in high places, especially with Democrats, elected Democrats in town, in Sacramento, and even in Washington. You want something done, donate to their charity and it gets done." Myrna was talking fast now. "Except for Negros, they don't like Negros. In Congress only the Democrats owned slaves. They run the Klan you know.

"Myrna, Mister Hearst is a Democrat." Stan laid a hand on Myrna's knee.

"Anyway, that's why they have the charity." Myrna spoke slower and lower.

"I don't know the Blanktons," Hearst assured them. He reached behind to pick up the glass. He sipped the whiskey, and then studied the glass as he slowly turned it in his hand. "I may have a man who can help you," Hearst said.

Morgan smiled. The Senator, a powerful ally, had joined the fight.

The young couple exchanged a few pleasantries with Morgan and Hearst and left a short time later. Morgan walked them down to the street where she called for a horse-drawn hackney. The light rain had stopped and, after seeing Stan and Myrna off, Morgan hailed a hack for herself. "Drive around and have me back here in one hour," she told the driver. She stepped into the carriage and settled in the seat.

Morgan peered out to the side, watching buildings pass by without really seeing them. The Senator's question, she'd answered it flippantly, truthfully, but only as a cover for the real reason, or reasons. Well, she asked herself, so why Stryker? Why him? She'd been married to Jack, her husband, fourteen years, or was it fifteen, before his murder in Bickford. Shouldn't she remember the years?

They'd married young, she had anyway. Sixteen for her, he was thirty-three. They soon had a son, Lucas. For some reason, they didn't try to have more children. Neither spoke about it. He stayed engulfed in his work, a self-taught mining engineer. When Lucas got older, Morgan accompanied Jack on his expeditions and they both came home exhausted. And home, during those first years, was a tent, a tent with three occupants, usually pitched near other tents. That could have been one reason for the infrequent love making, she thought. Okay, she had to admit, neither she nor Jack seemed all that interested. Duty is no substitute for passion.

Their success with the mines and ranching changed little. However, Jack and Morgan built a life together, a good one. A town sprang up around their mines and the cattle ranch. When it grew big enough, they named it Bickford. Then that gang murdered Jack, and renamed the town. Strange, she seemed to grieve more for the town than for Jack. Jack was a good man, though. Labored hard all his life, he asked only for twenty-four hours a day to work. They threw him down one of his own mine shafts.

The night she met Stryker, she offered her body to get herself and Lucas out of Egalitaria. When she got more than she bargained for, she'd tried to change her mind. Up until then, Jack had been the only man. Love making with him had always been . . . polite. Stryker wasn't polite. He saw what he wanted and took it, took her. The nervousness that night, the excitement, the . . . danger, still lingered vividly in her memory. They had fought and he'd thrown her on the bed, pinned her down. At first he used his hand, his fingers, as she struggled to free herself. But then, her struggles became less vigorous. A strange feeling began inside, growing, building, and it started to take over . . . a new sensation. The more it grew, the more it intensified, the faster she felt swept along, driving her toward an unknown. And then, suddenly, her body exploded in an eruption of pleasure, washing over her, starting in the small of her back, rushing up to tingle her scalp and down to curl her toes. Her back arched and she'd tried to sweep her arms down to the epicenter of pleasure but he held her wrists tightly against the head rails. As she'd laid there wondering what had just happened, he continued the rhythmic caressing, relentlessly, and she gradually sensed another approaching wave. And then another. More followed, and she realized he was *making* them happen! How stupid of her not to know that. But, these things had never happened before. How was she to know? Eventually, all she could do was to cling to him as he moved inside her, still touching her down there, causing more spasms of pleasure. It finally occurred to her, he was making her have those intense pleasures for *his own* benefit. He controlled her with them. She, a hard-assed woman, disciplined and determined, would, she decided, allow herself to be controlled this way. Why the hell not? Afterwards, when all was finished, she lay exhausted. That night she had lived, and when he comes back, if he comes back, she wanted to live again.

"Miss, Miss, we're back at the Palace." The hack driver said . . . politely.

Morgan deftly returned to the present. "Thank you, driver." She paid him and stepped from the carriage.

CHAPTER TEN

Riding south from Ogden proved frustrating to Stryker from early on. Oxen pulled the wagon slower than horses or mules, and Stryker suspected Montel was moving faster in the other wagons ahead. It took three long days to reach Salt Lake City. The trail ran south in between the Wasatch Mountains to the east and the Great Salt Lake to the west. They had the looming mountains, clearly visible, on their left, and occasionally they could glimpse slivers of lake water beyond the wide marshlands to their right.

Stryker made camp and ate his meals, away from the wagon. He moved farther out the first night. Jacob and the women held nightly services in the wagon. The praying, crying, and supplications got on his nerves. So, he sought distance from the religious rituals, searching for a dirt mound or some kind of natural barrier to help avoid the annoying sounds of worship. He was not invited to join them and that suited him.

Upon arriving in Salt Lake City, "Great" being dropped by many of the people living there, they learned the other group had waited a day and pushed on, still heading south through the Salt Lake Valley.

Several days passed and Stryker had enough of the slow progress. He tucked the roan in beside the wagon and asked, "Jacob, where the hell are you going?"

"Kanab, there's a fort there and a settlement. No need to cuss, sir."

"How long to reach it?"

"About ten more days if we don't have trouble. Utes and Paiutes, none too happy 'bout us coming down their valley." Jacob nodded at both Rebecca and Mabel, seated beside him. Mabel, who sat closest to Stryker, didn't catch the gesture. "That's why we're mighty grateful you're ridin' with us."

"This trail go to Kanab?"

"All the way. There's a river just ahead. We follow it through a long valley past Panguitch. It narrows to a stream and breaks west from the trail, a creek flowing down from the mountains. The trail continues south and picks up another creek to follow. I have friends in the United Order of Orderville. We can rest a day or two before pushing on to Kanab," Jacob said, confident he had impressed Stryker with his knowledge of the trail to Kanab.

Stryker heeled the roan's flanks.

Jacob and the women, including Alacrity who poked her head out from the Conestoga, watched the mixed-breed gallop off and eventually disappear, riding the trail into the mouth of a canyon. The four evidently figured that shouting pleas would be useless.

"Should we turn back?" Mabel asked.

"There's Mormon settlements along the creek," Jacob said. He drew in a deep breath and released a loud huff of resignation. "We'll ask them."

Stryker entered the Sevier River Canyon, which was more like a narrow valley because sparsely wooded, pinyon pine and juniper blanketed the hills rising up from the Sevier River. Cottonwood trees, lining each bank, showed where the water meandered through the valley. The river flowed north. Feeder streams flowed into it from the mountains, and it ran swollen due to a recent rain. Twilight approached and it'd been a good three hours since he'd left Jacob and the women. The north section of the canyon wasn't very wide, leaving barely enough room for the trail and river, but now it began to broaden. Ahead he saw a big yellow hill rising above the trees. He also saw smoke.

He rounded a curve in the trail, and a came upon a large green meadow. Instead of seeing dwellings of a Mormon settlement on the valley floor, he saw tipis, some with animal skins painted with berry juice, sewn together and stretched over poles, wide at the base, narrow at the top and lashed together to form the cones. He estimated there were more than thirty spread out on the grassy meadow between the river and the yellow hill. Smoke curled upward from smoldering fires in front of each dwelling. He saw Indian men and women, some with children promenading with purpose. Paiutes, he reckoned, seemed to all be moving toward a large, vacant grassy area, encircled by the tipis. They were all outfitted in ceremonial dress with colorful feathers and beads sewn into buckskin shirts and leggings. The trail ran right through the tipis, with some on his left, by the river. Most of the encampments were on flat ground to his right, surrounding the open space of grass.

Stryker's intentions were to continue riding the trail, past the Paiutes. He eased the roan forward, stopping, at times, to let Indians cross in front of him. Few of them looked his way, and those who did, did so with casual, non-threatening, glances. He'd almost gotten by the last of the tipis when several braves came up from behind, seemingly from nowhere. Two of them moved to both sides of the roan's head so quickly Stryker had no time to spur its flanks before they each had grasped the roan's bridle. A third Paiute positioned himself by Stryker's stirrup.

"The Chief of Paiute invite you to Dance of Sun," the brave by the stirrup said sternly. "He send Puku to bring you."

Stryker glanced to his rear and saw four more Paiutes directly behind the roan with bows drawn.

Puku noted his hesitancy. "Great chief Tutzegubet say you guest. Come."

Stryker swung from the saddle and stepped forward, looping the reins over the roan's head. "I'll lead him," Stryker said, shoving himself between the roan and one of the two Paiutes holding the bridle. A nod from the English-speaking Puku, and both Paiutes let go of the bridle and backed away from Stryker and his horse. Puku turned and started toward the open area. Stryker followed with the roan, and the rest of the braves fell in behind the big horse.

The tall mixed-breed towered at least a foot taller than the Paiutes. Now, as he walked among the tribe, he garnered looks from its members, who seeing him join them engendered curiosity. Stryker saw the man he assumed to be the chief as he reached the grassy field. The leader sat in a padded rocking chair, wearing a many-feathered headdress that trailed down behind the chair. His fringed tunic, made from deer hide, was adorned with beads that spread across his chest in white rows, and beaded animal shapes in red, blue, and yellow were sewn into his sleeves. He rocked slowly back and forth, watching Stryker approach. The chair, maybe given to him from settlers, or stolen, seemed to provide much pleasure to Tutzegubet.

"I take horse. Chief not like on sacred ground," Puku quietly warned Stryker. He held out his hand for the reins. Stryker passed them to him and the brave, in turn, handed them off to one of the trailing braves.

"Keep him in my sight," Stryker ordered, throwing a hard look at the English-speaking Paiute.

Puku said something to the other braves Stryker couldn't understand; however, the roan was tied to a small tree not far away.

Stryker and Puku halted in front of the chief, who continued to rock his chair. He spoke Paiute to Stryker, ending the words with, *"Mormon."*

"He asked if you're Mormon. Mormons try stop Sun Dance," Puku explained. "We come down canyon, so be left alone. Chief not friend of Mormons. They kill Paiute women and children many years ago in Black Hawk war. But, he still has much anger. You Mormon?"

"No."

The chief spoke again, this time his words ended with, "Ute."

"You Ute?" Puku asked.

Stryker shook his head.

"Utes steal our women, horses. You have Indian blood in veins?"

Stryker figured his straight black hair, tanned skin, must have prompted the question. His mother did have slight native born ancestry, in addition to Asian and Anglo-Saxon. The father hailed from Scandinavia. However, he thought he was more likely, part Hispanic, which he was. "Some maybe, Asian and white too, I reckon." Indian blood would be more welcome than Mexican, he reasoned. He'd heard of the Circleville massacre too. Not the Mormon's finest hour he remembered, but there were wrongs on both sides, and life was hard then, even more than today.

Tutzegubet, still rocking, lifted an arm and swept it from Stryker to the ground beside him. Puku sat as well, positioning himself between and behind Stryker and the chief.

Poles, with their tops wrapped in tarred cloth, and planted around the grassy area, were lit by young boys running from pole to pole carrying fire. Although not quite dark, the lighting signaled the beginning of the festivities.

An elderly male moved to the center of the Paiutes who had seated themselves on the grass. He remained standing and began to sing, chanting really, with a monotone cadence. Members of the tribe, who had been seated, rose and walked to the edge of the grass, where they started shuffling in a slow circular, dance. Another old brave, a shaman or medicine man, his long white hair hanging down past his shoulders, began singing and pounding a drumstick made with balled rawhide. He beat rhythmically on a buckskin drum held between his knees. The dancers kept time by stepping with each drumbeat, and dipping their bodies on every fourth beat. Males and females joined in, making a wide circle around the shaman.

"Mormons brought drum,' Puku said. The chief kept on with his rocking. But Stryker figured he heard Puku talking and knew some of the words. "They bring many things to Paiute people; drum, rocking chair, food, God we not see, words on paper, and sick death they call "Calra." Stryker understood that to mean "cholera."

"Do they steal your women?" Stryker asked. The one time Stryker used humor, he purposely tried it on a man who wouldn't get it.

"No, they have too many women. Must share man. Paiute have just one. Ute want be like Mormon. But only take young and pretty ones. We left with old and ugly." Puku ruefully surveyed the dancers. "Tribe get small."

Stryker, Chief Tutzegubet, and Puku watched the dancers in silence for a long hour, causing Stryker to wonder why the chief had him brought to the celebration. He did speculate, however, if he'd been Mormon or Ute, the Paiutes may not have been as friendly. He guessed Tutzegubet might be trying to decide what to do with him.

Stryker spent most of the hour working on an escape plan and getting back to his mission.

A loud commotion of shouts in English and Paiute, erupted from behind the tipis, and Stryker leapt to his feet. Several dancers stopped, causing others to bump into them. They turned their attention to the rukus. Dancing ceased, and the drum fell silent. The chief stopped his rocking.

From around one of the tipis, Jacob and the three women, each with braves on either side, emerged moving toward Stryker and the chief, Jacob in the lead. He didn't struggle. The women, especially Alacrity, fought mightily with their Paiute captors. Alacrity spotted Stryker and she somehow wrenched herself free to bolt forward and make a desperate dash across the meadow.

"Stryker! Stryker!" She cried, and running as fast as she could, the ends of her white dress bounced on her knees. The Paiutes recaptured her before she made it halfway. "Let me go to my husband!"

Chief Tutzegubet raised an arm, palm facing toward himself, signaling for the braves to release Alacrity and allow her to come on.

She broke into another run straight toward Stryker. "Stryker! You're here! And safe!" She threw her arms around him and kissed his face all before burying her own face in his shoulder and sobbing. She held on so fiercely, he didn't try to pry her loose.

"She your woman?" Puku asked?

Alacrity tore her head away from Stryker's shoulder. "Yes, I'm his WOMAN! I'm his wife!" She looked up at him. "Honey, can we go, can we leave here? Please?"

The chief spoke Paiute to Puku.

"Chief say you stay, sit, watch dance. We have game, contest, later." After seeing hesitation on the faces of Alacrity and Jacob, who had just walked up, he warned, "It demand, really."

"Sit," Stryker ordered. "Enjoy the celebration. It's bad to be rude."

Taking a cue from the mixed-breed, who they'd come to know was not given to idle talk, Jacob and the women sat, drawing a big smile of relief on Puku.

The shaman resumed his drumbeat and dancers shifted their attention back to the shuffling, stepping in place as the circle of

Paiutes gradually resumed its rotation. The chanting started in again, the singer turning at times to watch the dancing.

After two hours, or so, of chanting and dancing, Chief Tutzegubet lifted an arm and the music stopped. The dancers all dropped to a cross-legged seated position, facing the now quiet singer. Night had taken command of the evening and the only light came from the torches ringing the ceremonial ground.

"Now is time for game, contest of skill and courage," Puku leaned over to tell Stryker. "Two men see who first draw blood. One called Tooonug, which mean tooonugwetsedu, or big cat of mountain. He very fast. Cut deep with knife. Others not like fight with him. He here tonight."

Two young Piautes appeared at opposite sides of the circle. Stryker had not seen where they came from. He suspected they'd been resting in tipis, waiting for a break in the dancing. They looked to be in their early teens but stood bravely as any man among the gathering. The shaman spread both arms, stretching his hands out toward the two contestants. He then crossed his forearms across his chest, and the two boys walked to the center, each with a knife stuck in the red cloths tied around their waists. The shaman stepped aside and the boys faced off, knives drawn.

At first, the young combatants warily circled one another, making half-hearted knife thrusts. Eventually, their blades got closer, snagging a rawhide sleeve or a flapping shirt tail. Each close call emboldened the recipient to be more daring with his own thrust. The drumming resumed and sporadic shouts from the Paiutes encouraged the fighters. Finally, one of them made a long stabbing jab at his opponent's stomach, who tried to block the move with his knife hand, thus cutting the stabber's hand. It was shallow cut, but enough to end the fight, much to the relief of the two boys. They jogged from the ring with both combatants' arms in the air, one boy in victory and the other youngster showing off his wound.

Two braves began to chant "Tooonug, Tooonug." Seated Paiute dancers, now joined by tribe members who had not danced peered anxiously around, searching for the warrior Tooonug. But he did not show. Another brave emerged from a tipi at the far end of the ceremonial ground, from Chief Tutzegubet. Like the boys earlier, he waited. Older than the prior combatants, although not much older, he seemed mature enough to present more of a challenge against Tooonug. The chanting for him grew louder, but still, no Tooonug.

Puku leaned over to Stryker. "He Johnson Half-Bear. He live with white family since boy. Come to Sun Dance. Go back after. "

Chief Tutzegubet nodded to the shaman. The shaman lifted his arms to silence the Paiutes. And, after the last call for the fearsome warrior died away, he dropped an arm and pointed at a tipi with the image of a mountain lion on it. He called out, "Tooonug!"

Then, Tooonug emerged from his tipi, standing proud, and confident. Like the other members of his tribe, he was short, no more than five feet, four inches tall. Yet, he seemed bigger because of the way he carried himself. He stood straight, stretching his short frame up to its maximum height, and remained motionless while he soaked up the tribe's rousing whoops and bellows. His facial features were chiseled, prominent cheekbones, mouth a straight fixed line. When he started his march to the center, it seemed as if he condescended to do it. However, he acknowledged his opponent with a nod, as if to recognize the challenger's bravery.

The shaman simply stepped away, as the signal for the fight to begin.

The two fighters warily circled each other. No fake thrusts, the two were serious. The challenger, taller than Tooonug, held his knife handle as in a hand shake, tip pointed toward Tooonug, in order to thrust it. Tooonug gripped the knife blade down his forearm. His tactic was to move in close and slash. Tooonug sought not just to draw blood and win. He aimed to punish.

For five long minutes they circled. Then, Tooonug drew his blade hand back to his right ear, and Johnson Half Bear saw an opening. He slid his right foot forward and thrust the knife point at the left shoulder of Tooonug. But the crafty warrior swept his right foot behind the left and spun his body completely around, extending and swinging his knife arm in a wide arc. The blade entered beneath Johnson Half-Bear's cheek bone, slashed diagonally across his face, and exited his mouth. Tooonug raised both arms, blood dripping from the blade, in triumph. The young brave, holding his cheek flap, watched Tooonug parade around the circle of Paiutes. Johnson Half Bear made his way to his tipi, presumably to be attended to by a waiting squaw using a bone needle and horse-hair thread.

Tooonug flaunted his victory with two leisurely victory laps before retiring into his own tipi.

Stryker watched the shaman move to the center and begin his chants with a renewed drumbeat. Then, as dancers rose to their feet and resumed the rhythmic shuffling, he leaned over to Puku. "How long do they dance?"

"Dance til light."

"We must leave soon!" Jacob had heard Puku's reply. He pointed at Rebecca. "Her husband expects her in Fort Kanab. He's the Captain there with seventy soldiers." Jacob scooted closer to Puku. "We're with those wagons that just came through here. They'll be stopping in Orderville to wait for us.

"You Mormon?" Puku asked. "Those other wagons, they were Mormon?"

Upon hearing the word *"Mormon"*, the Chief turned his attention from the dancing to Jacob and Puku.

"Not anymore." Jacob shook his head no. He hoped that answer was the right one. Then, he gambled big. "You don't want another Circleville."

Puku's face darkened. He swung around to Chief Tutzengubet. The two had hurried exchanges in their own language. Finally, the old Chief looked at Jacob and straightened himself in the chair he'd stopped rocking, to announce what appeared to be his decision.

Puku stoically repeated his leader's words. "Chief say, 'you are welcome to stay tonight, but in morning you must go'."

The valley had begun to shred its nighttime cloak when Stryker decided it was safe to leave the Paiutes. A gray dawn was creeping in and the dancing had stopped. All but a few of the dancers had retired to their tipis and those still outside on the grass, slumbered where they sat. Chief Tutzengubet snored in his rocker. From what Stryker could tell only Puku, Stryker, Jacob, and the women remained awake,

Puku said nothing, nor did he stir, when he saw Stryker tap Jacob on his shoulder and point toward their wagon. Puku and Stryker exchanged quick glances before the tall man got to his feet, and then Puku remained sitting cross-legged, staring straight ahead.

Stryker made his way over to the roan, where it stood, still tied to a cottonwood. It welcomed the man who'd ridden its back for years with a nicker. He untied the reins and ducked under the horse's neck to check on the Winchester and found Tooonug waiting for him.

"Tooonug horse." The Paiute pointed the tip of the knife blade at Stryker's face.

Stryker worked his hand around to the sai as he straightened. The menacing weapon flashed in a blur as he flipped it. He gripped it with the handle in his fist, needle sharp tips down his forearm. Stryker dropped lower, spread his feet, left foot in front, and left hand forward in an eagle claw, the other hand readied the sai by his shoulder.

Tooonug was feared, respected by some, and not well liked. However, he was no fool. He backed around the roan's rear, and melted into the trees.

Stryker figured Tooonug chose not to risk his reputation by alerting the tribe.

Stryker led the roan down to the river and let it drink. When the big horse had drunk a sufficient amount of water, he pulled on the head stall, and walked it back up to the trail where he met Jacob leading the oxen and wagon. Rebecca, Mabel, and Alacrity walked alongside as well. Neither man spoke. Stryker led the roan at a faster clip until he was two hundred paces ahead and then he slowed, maintaining the gap between him and the wagon.

A few minutes went by and Stryker heard footfalls coming up from behind. He turned around to see Alacrity. She walked with her head down, trying not to trip, but looked up and smiled when Stryker noticed her. She ran the last few feet to catch up.

"I pretended you were my husband because . . ."

"I know why you did it," Stryker groused.

Alacrity fell silent for several minutes and then she asked, "Would you like to join us the next time we cleanse the devil?"

Even though Stryker's curiosity was piqued at the thought of bathing the bane of mankind, he kept it to himself. "No."

'I guess I misspoke," she giggled. "I didn't intend to mean we clean the devil. We clean *ourselves* of the devil." She swiped her hands down the sides of her torso as in a washing motion. "We wash him out of our bodies. That's what we do some nights. I don't know, but you may have heard us. Did you?"

"Uh-huh."

"Sorry. Sometimes it's hard to get him out."

"Alacrity, what the hell are you talking about?"

"Don't you ever have bad thoughts? And you know it's the work of the devil?" She got nothing from the man next to her. "Well, I'm sure you do. We all do." She paused again, and then went on. "Jacob learned us how to get rid of the devil, get him out of our bodies."

With that, Stryker glanced at the girl. He looked impassive. However, the look did invite more from the naïve girl with poor grammar.

"When one of us lets the devil in during the day, then at night, Jacob has us take off our clothing and he gets him out of you. Not just Jacob, the others help too," she quickly added.

"You're shitin' me."

"You said a bad word, but that's okay. The 'book' says 'Satan, get thee away from me,' and that's what we do." Alacrity nodded her head vigorously. She saw him look sideways at her. "No, it works Stryker!" She gestured with her hands again. "You can tell when the devil leaves you. It feels wonderful!"

"Jesus."

"That's better." Alacrity took that as Stryker invoking the almighty to confirm the authenticity of their religious experience. Emboldened, she continued. "We lay down and everyone puts their hands on you. Usually Jacob touches me below, down there." She pointed. Stryker didn't have to look to know where she meant. "The others, Rebecca and Mabel, rub me up here." Again, he figured correctly. "Jacob knows just how to do it. When the devil starts to come out, it feels really good. And when he does come all the way out, there's a wondrous feeling, a sensation, Stryker, that washes all over me. I guess that's why I said cleansing before. Sometimes the devil sneaks back in and it takes several cleansings to finally get him out. And that old Satan, he takes a awful beatin'."

Stryker started to say something but before he could find the words, Alacrity continued. "Sometimes Jacob has to use the staff of life. He sticks it inside and pulls the devil into it, and then we use our hands on it, to get the devil out that way. I wish you'd join us. I feel Satan in me now."

"No thanks. I really don't know much about the good book, but now I'll sure do more reading."

"Are you gonna leave us again?"

"Yes."

"Why?"

"After a man."

"Is he good or bad?"

"Bad. Been chasing the cocksucker three weeks."

"What's a cocksucker?"

"A man who doesn't keep his word," Stryker said, as he looped the reins over the roan's ears, and swung into the saddle. He dug in his heels and started the horse off at an easy gait. He was almost out of earshot when he heard Alacrity's shout of good wishes.

"Hope you find that cocksucker!"

CHAPTER ELEVEN

Stryker never took another's council on religion, nor did he offer it. He figured the unknowable was also unteachable. Each to his own, except those religions where sinners are put to the rack or have their heads cut off. Those who can only feel righteous by making people suffer should be shot. Jacob and the women seem to enjoy their beliefs, and what the hell, they weren't hurting anybody. None of his business.

He sighted the trail ahead between the roan's ears. He liked seeing the world from that view. Fresh air on a clear morning, creaking saddle leather, and an occasional snort from the horse under him— damn, that's good shit. Presently, the canyon opened up to a wide valley, with green, grassy meadows sloping upward from the river to heavily wooded mountains on his right, and red sandstone cliffs to his left. A small buffalo herd grazed in the lush grass beneath the sandstone, along with three mule deer–bucks with early season racks who seemed oblivious to the huge beasts not more than fifty yards away. A ferruginous hawk sailed in the clear blue sky, searching for a fresh rodent breakfast. The vivid colors, green, blue, and red, made it look as though the valley had been painted by a giant artist. It was the kind of day a man wouldn't ever want taken away from him.

Still, he had a job to do. It's about time he caught up with Montel and got the cocksucker to sign the deed.

He'd skirted the small settlement of Panguitch on purpose, no more delays. He made camp at day's end, a few hundred yards up a feeder creek to the river, not wishing to be within earshot of Jacob and the women's devil purging, in case they caught up with him. They didn't though, and the following morning, after a quick breakfast of coffee and a biscuit, he got back on the trail south. He'd camped near a stream that flowed down from the mountains to the Sevier River and he rode upstream beside it until it veered up out of the valley. He crested a long gentle rise and began to follow along a new creek down the far side. The valley narrowed again, both sides heavily wooded, and the trail hugged the rushing stream. Late afternoon brought Stryker to a settlement called Orderville.

A teenage boy approached Stryker as he fed and watered the roan, engaging him with a history of the Order. He bragged about how the group had formed a commune of around three hundred Mormons, and that they practiced collectivism, although he didn't call it that. Everyone worked and turned over the fruits of their labor to the Order, and the leaders redistributed everything, he said.

"You're welcome to stay and join us," the boy offered.

"No thanks, I had enough of that shit in Egalitaria."

"Sir, you don't have to talk like . . .," the youngster began.

"Give it some time, you'll call it what it is." Stryker climbed on the roan and rode off.

He made camp five miles farther down the trail after passing a makeshift sign, painted in faded white letters, for Zion Canyon, with an arrow pointing to a narrow trail that wound uphill. Stryker figured the westward path was likely made by Indians, Paiutes probably, looking for game or higher ground in the summer. The stream widened to a good-sized creek and he built a fire nearby the shallows just before nightfall. Since there was no sign of Jacob and the women, he figured he'd probably put too many miles between them or they'd stopped in Orderville. Kanab, a small newly-formed ward for the Mormons, still lay fifteen miles south. He wanted to be on the trail way before sun up. The daytime temperature had been rising as he rode south and would likely top 100 degrees by midday. Red sandstone now dominated the landscape and shade looked to be scarce. He fed and watered the roan, then had beans and salted pork for dinner and washed it down with black coffee. He slept on top of his bedroll and used his saddle for a pillow.

Stars sparkled brightly in the clear sky and a full moon lit the campsite in relatively lustrous light when Stryker threw the bedroll on the roan at three in the morning. He followed the trail along a sandy wash until the wagon tracks split off, turning east and leading up a long winding rise in elevation, topping out near six-thousand feet. At the crest, the view opened up to a panoramic view of the high desert with towering red cliffs in the distance, but Stryker pressed on without slowing to enjoy it. Although he couldn't yet see Kanab, he figured once he descended a few miles, he'd get to the town. In another hour, he came to Kanab creek and, after letting his horse take water, he followed the creek to the edge of the Mormon settlement.

It took several tries, mainly due to hostile Indians, but finally Kanab had taken root and now had around four hundred inhabitants. Stryker rode into the dusty little town, wondering why in hell Montel chose to flee all the way here and hole up with Mormons. Riding down the main street he garnered wary looks from men in black suits and heavy beards, and women in prairie dresses and bonnets. Presently, he came to a telegraph office and reined in the roan.

"Looking for a Frenchman," Stryker announced, coming in the door.

The bearded man standing behind a counter resembling a bank window snapped his head up from separating a pile of papers. He studied the face of the man who'd just walked in and decided not to antagonize him. The .44 slung low on the man's hip looked well-used and his fearsome countenance warned it wouldn't require much to put it in action. "Haven't seen one, mister. Might be with the wagons that arrived here yesterday, though." The telegraph operator fumbled nervously with the papers but kept his eyes on the mixed-breed.

"Wagons still here." Stryker had a habit of asking questions with a statement.

"Believe so. South edge of town." The wireman elected to be brief as well.

Stryker turned for the door. It opened before his hand touched the knob. In came a clean shaven, small of frame, and wiry, younger man.

Dark hair and brilliant obsidian eyes, he could have easily looked fierce with a beard. He appeared to be in his late twenties but the smooth tan face could have been the reason the years seemed so friendly. The man cast a watchful glance at Stryker and approached the counter.

"*Je veux envoyer un telegramme.*"

"Sir, I don't . . ."

Stryker whirled. "You, get out." He pulled the .44, pointed its barrel at the telegraph operator. The operator backed away, spun around, and rushed out the rear door. Stryker gripped the Frenchman by the collar and dragged him backwards to the small table used for composing wires. He pulled the *Examiner's* deed from his shirt pocket as he jammed the Frenchman into the chair. Slamming the deed on the table, he reached for pen and ink through the window's bars, all the while keeping the Peacemaker trained on the Frenchman. He set the writing material in front of him. "Sign it, Montel."

The Frenchman frantically shook his head no.

Stryker thumbed the Colt's hammer. He intended his shot to shatter the man's shoulder but his hand jerked at the last minute by what he heard and the bullet grazed the arm. It wasn't the shrill voice that caused his hand to twitch, but rather what was said.

"They'll kill my husband!"

"Aw, God-dammit." Stryker lowered the Peacemaker and grabbed a fist full of hair, short hair, which he now recognized as crudely cut. He pulled the woman from the chair and slammed her against the wall. He threw his hand around her throat, keeping her pinned upright. She choked, struggling to breathe, and clawed at his hand, trying to pry it loose. His face full of rage was inches from the woman's. He held her there until her eyes fluttered together and her body began to sag. Stryker released her neck and gripped a clump of hair, jamming fist and hair against the wall. The pain in her scalp revived her and she tried to scream. A slap across the face stuffed it back down her throat.

"I'm kind of mad at you."

She spoke through gritted teeth. "My husband was supposed to be here but he fell and broke his back. You can figure the rest." She spoke English with a heavy accent. Her voice sounded raspy, husky, a masculine tone for a woman.

"That God-Damned Montel's still in San Francisco," Stryker suddenly realized. He released her throat. "Why are you here?"

"I tried to get as far as . . ." She felt her arm and pulled it away to look at the blood.

"The wire office dammit!" Stryker, angry at her and at himself for being so easily fooled, blasted out the words.

"I'm at the end here. I was gonna tell 'em you got killed by Indians. Didn't know what else to do. Can't believe you followed me all the way . . . you gonna kill me?"

"Haven't decided. You got a name?" Stryker growled.

"Cossette, Cossette Affair."

"Of course it is."

"Well?" Cossette stiffened her body, sat up straight, held her breath.

"Send the telegram."

"Are you going back to San Francisco?" The woman relaxed enough to breathe.

"Yes."

"Take me with you. Don't leave me here with them. They already suspect I'm a woman. I don't want to be one of their wives. Please." The husky voice grew plaintive.

"No. Send the telegram." He spun around and threw open the door.

Outside, the telegraph operator was coming up the street with two men, and even a hundred feet away, they looked big and stout. Stryker grabbed the reins and swung atop the roan. He pulled the big horse away from the rail and spurred it to an easy canter, heading north back out of Kanab. The ride down to town had made for a long day and he'd have to pull off the trail and make camp soon.

Once out of town, he let the roan walk, the grade slight, but noticeable, up through the sandstone canyon. He trailed along Kanab creek lost in thought, recriminations really, of his own stupidity. Whether the money, or the woman, he'd lost focus on the task, failed to reason things out, and he should have figured he was being led away from Montel. He'd chased the money and the woman, not Montel.

The entire damn trip had been a colossal waste of time, he told himself. The girl, or woman, or whatever the hell she was, had run, run hard, and not with any kind of plan. But in her desperation to escape from him, she'd tried to hide with Mormon renegades and had gotten herself trapped. She couldn't run out of Kanab by herself, and eventually they were bound to find out she couldn't piss standing up. Serves her right. However, he was angrier with himself than at her. Being made a fool of is about the worst kind of injury a man can have. Five miles on the trail hadn't eased his sour mood and the ride back to San Francisco probably wouldn't ease it either. Shit.

He reined the roan toward the creek which had begun to play out below steeper terrain and dismounted. Sandstone walls over a hundred feet in height crowded in forming a canyon he would rise out of in a few miles. Stryker refilled his canteen while the horse sucked in the cool water. The stream barely trickled out from a spring here. The water ran fresh and cool, probably the last remnants of snow melt percolating off higher elevations.

The sound of clopping hooves behind him snapped Stryker out of his angry brooding. Far down the trail, he saw her slapping the sides of a horse which, even at a distance, he could see was lathered and laboring. By the time Cossette reached him, the horse was struggling to stay upright. She remained seated in the saddle, breathing hard, as if she'd made the run on foot.

"How far back are they?" Stryker grasped the horse's head stall and led it to the stream. He let the horse drink a few gulps and then then with considerable effort, pulled its muzzle away from the creek. "Get off. How far back?" He grabbed her hat off her head and dipped it in the water. Cossette stretched out her hands to take it, but Stryker poured the water over the neck of her horse, swiping down the lather with his hand. "I said how far back."

"I don't know, a mile I guess. I only saw 'em once. We should get going"

"How many?" Stryker poured another hatful on the horse.

"Them two men with the tele . . . I'm thirsty too!"

"You steal the mare?"

"I saw it out back and I took it. And yes, I crawled through the counter window to get out the back door," Cossette said, as she got on fours, and leaned over to drink from the creek. She pulled her face from the water long enough to say, "I can take you to Montel." Then she drank more water.

"Four of 'em."

"Huh?" Cossette lifted her face, water running off her chin.

"There's four men coming." Stryker pulled the .44-40 off the roan. He chambered a shell and handed the Winchester to Cossette. "Can you shoot it?"

She nodded yes.

"Just hold it. Don't fire unless I do." Stryker tied both horses to a shrub pine and then moved several paces away. He left the Peacemaker holstered. Cossette shadowed Stryker and stood with him near a head high sandstone boulder as they waited for the approaching riders.

The riders allowed their mounts to slow and then halt completely on their own. All four carried shotguns. They were the two men Stryker had seen walking toward the telegraph office, the telegraph operator, and another new man.

"Evening mister," the wireman said, with a fake smile that danced nervously on his face. "This here's Levi, Heth, and Amos. They're my cousins. I'm Ezekiel." The four men dismounted, keeping a watchful on Stryker as they slid from the saddles. "Hot and dusty ride," Ezekiel said.

The men led their horses to the creek. They mumbled to themselves while getting water and afterwards, straightened with decisive purpose. They stepped away from the horses. Stryker sensed they'd become more determined. His muscles tensed, nerves pumping adrenalin.

"That horse was stolen," Levi, largest of the four grunted, pointing at the mare with the gun barrel.

"Reckon so," Stryker allowed.

"We'd like her back."

"How much for a horse," Stryker countered.

"What you offering?" Levi shouldered the conversation.

101

"A hundred."

The four men cast sideways glances at each other, grinning, possibly thinking the stranger carried more than the hundred and needed to be relieved of it.

Heth asked, "She your woman?"

"I'm his wife," Cossette answered curtly.

"She ain't his wife. They didn't even know one another when they come in my office. You could tell." The wireman angrily asserted.

"We'll be takin' her back too. Need five . . ."

"Like hell you will!" Cossette raised the .44-.40 and fired.

The large caliber round hit Amos in the groin. His free hand went to his crotch as he struggled to raise the 12-gauge in his other hand. He pulled the trigger too soon and the blast blew a crater in the dirt a few feet past his boots.

The crack of the Winchester followed by the roar of the shotgun caught the other three men by surprise, and it took a moment for them to realize what had just happened. Heth recovered the quickest and he brought his double-barrel up to level it. For just a split second, he was indecisive in picking his target, Cossette, who had started the shooting, or the tall man next to her. By the time he'd made his decision, it was too late. Stryker's bullet slammed into his chest, left of center.

Ezekiel fumbled with the shotgun as though he'd never used it. A second round from the Peacemaker drilled into his gut and he threw his gun to the ground in anger. He turned to take a few wavering steps toward his horse but sank to his knees.

Cossette rapidly pulled the Winchester's trigger in a futile effort to fire. She'd forgotten to work the lever.

Strangely, Levi never attempted to raise his shotgun. He stood erect and motionless, looking straight ahead, seemingly oblivious to the gunfire. Slowly, very slowly, he began to lean forward. Similar to a giant redwood being felled, his big body gathered speed as the angle between his frame and the ground closed, and he crashed to the ground in a cloud of dust. An arrow, sunk deeply between Levi's shoulder blades, remained starkly vertical.

Stryker looked beyond the dying Levi to see Tooonug step out from behind one of the large boulders. He held his bow in one hand with no arrow strung. Stryker kept his Colt pointed away from him as he strode over to, first Amos, where he fired a bullet into the back of his head, and then to Ezekiel, ending his misery as well. In the meantime, Levi died.

"They weren't regular Mormons," Cossette said, staring at the dead men. "The others treated me well. Not these ones."

Stryker laid the four bodies in stacks of twos, tied their legs together using ropes from the other horses, and dragged the bodies to a dry gulch, out of sight. Tooonug stood silently watching. When Stryker finished he walked up to him.

"You know our tongue?"

Tooonug nodded that he did.

"We take two horses, you take four," Stryker said.

"Agreed."

The Paiute warrior and Stryker divided the horses. Stryker took the reins of the roan and pulled another horse from the four by the creek, giving Tooonug Cossette's horse without objection from the Paiute. The Paiute took one shotgun to carry and lashed the others behind the saddle of the horse he'd chosen to ride. He then swung onto his mount without using the stirrup.

"Follow," Tooonug said, and he started up the trail, leading the three roped horses behind him. In less than a hundred paces, he leapt from the lead horse and ran to a cluster of trees near the wash. He returned leading his own pony. Instead of riding it, though, he roped it with the other three, and climbed back on the horse he'd been riding.

Stryker and Cossette waited as Tooonug retrieved his mount and took up the trail again.

"Why's he helping us?" Cossette asked.

"He'll be a hero to the tribe, riding in with four horses."

"Why not six horses?"

Stryker paused and answered. "We've met before. Reckon you had good reason to shoot that man's balls off."

"*Qui*, I was aiming at *monsieur* who does talking. Those bastards tried to lay with me even if they think I am a boy. I stay away from 'em. But no telling what would happen to me if I am woman." After a brief pause she said, "I'll bet *Monsieur* Indian saw you kill the men. Perhaps that's why he's agreeable."

After three hours of riding, Stryker yelled, "Tooonug, we camp here!" They'd come to where Stryker had camped the night before. The long day, the heat, the climb, and the shooting left him ready for a rest.

Tooonug preferred to spread his blanket on ground near the canyon wall, some distance away from Stryker and Cossette. Soon Tooonug had a small camp fire flickering and Stryker could see the Paiute's shadow on the sandstone when he stepped between the fire and the cliff wall.

Stryker built his own fire. He made coffee and threw a salted pork rind into the pot of beans he'd placed on two flat rocks over the glowing embers. He left the fire and tended to the horses, returning several minutes later to check on the cooking. Kneeling by the fire, he spooned out some of the beans on a tin plate and handed it and a fork to Cossette. The pot and a spoon, he set next to himself.

"We'll have to share the coffee cup."

Before trying the beans, she said, "I only planned to go as far as Salt Lake. Those men kidnapped me, brought me down this way, if that makes any difference." Cossette sat on the ground with the plate resting atop her crossed legs.

"You Cajun?"

"*Qui,* we sometimes worked in Montel's house. Our French is good enough. Look, what do they call you?

"Stryker"

"Look, *Monsieur* Stryker, they will kill Claude, my husband. Two of Montel's men, brutes named Jack and Shorty, they hold him. If you go back alive, Montel say they slit his throat."

"They're gone."

"Gone? You mean dead? You killed them?"

"One of 'em. The other one left the country."

Cossette glared Stryker for a moment, and then suddenly asked, "Who the hell are you?"

"You said you could get me Montel."

"And you'll help me save Claude, find him, keep them from killing him."

"I find Montel. He'll tell me where your husband is."

"Don't kill him before he tells you. I've seen how you finish things." Cossette waited for a reply that didn't come. "I'll pay you. I have ten dollars. We have forty more hidden in our home."

"Keep your money, Cossette. Montel can talk while he writes his name."

Cossette studied Stryker's face, what she could see of it, lit by the dying camp fire. "Those lines in your face, they're not laugh lines?"

Stryker swung around, untied the tarp and blanket from the saddle behind him, and tossed the blanket to Cossette. "You can use the blanket. I'll throw the tarp over there," Stryker said, pointing at the other side of the fire. "The other horses don't have bedrolls."

Long after the fire had died out, Stryker, lying on the tarp, woke up and quietly slipped his hand around the butt of the .44 by his chest. Years of sleeping lightly, seemingly always half-awake with senses never fully at rest, alerted him someone was nearby. Just he was about to pull and cock the Colt, he heard . . . "I'm cold." It was Cossette.

He eased the .44 back into place. She lay down beside him and stretched out the blanket over both of them. A little while later, he felt Cossette back up to him, and pull his arm around her.

The following morning they drank coffee from the same cup again. "I got cold, couldn't sleep, that's all," Cossette said, staring into the steaming cup. "How can it be so damn hot during the day and freezing cold at night?"

"Over a mile high here."

"Spent my entire life at sea level, guess I'm not used to this." Cossette looked beyond Stryker and the campfire. "Here comes that Indian with his horses." She handed the half empty cup to Stryker.

He drank the coffee in one large gulp and rinsed the cup in a small pot of hot water by the fire. "Let's go."

Once again Tooonug assumed the lead, his newly acquired horses trailing behind the proud owner. Holding the four ropes in one hand and brandishing the shotgun in the other, Tooonug seemingly had elevated himself to the station of a rich man. He kept the pace at a slow walk, making it easier to manage the four animals.

After several difficult miles up the trail toward Orderville, and without running into Jacob and his "wives", Stryker suspected they'd lingered a day or two in the communal Mormon town. However, that scenario didn't sit right with him. In order to secure statehood, the Mormons had eschewed polygamy and he doubted Jacob and his harem would have been welcomed in their town. Maybe, they hadn't stopped in Orderville.

The valley widened and the trail no longer hugged the creek. Grassy meadows carpeted the valley's floor between the trail, which ran along the base of mountains to the west, and the meandering creek flowing south, by the hills to the east. Stryker and Cossette stayed about a hundred paces behind Tooonug and the five horses, allowing for dust to settle, some of which did.

Up ahead, Stryker saw the Paiute stop and point his shotgun eastward, toward the hills. Stryker rode up to see why Tooonug stopped. In the distance, maybe a half mile away, stood what remained of a wagon, its canopy gone, the rest of it blackened and still smoldering.

"What's that?" Cossette asked.

"Probably, a dead man, and three dead women," Stryker replied.

"Shouldn't we go see?"

"No."

Stryker motioned for Tooonug to move on. Cossette dug in her heels, taking off toward the smoldering wagon. His first inclination was to let the foolish woman go, then he remembered her pledge on Montel. "Shit," he cursed under his breath and rode after her. He could have caught up and brought her back but decided not to. Tooonug trailed behind, keeping his mount at a walk.

Cossette got to the wagon first and saw the four bodies. The women lay on the wagon floor, neatly lying face down, all in a row. Jacob sat slumped on the seat facing them, several arrows jutting from his back, and part of his scalp cut away. The oxen were gone.

Stryker came up next to Cossette, who had chosen not to dismount and get closer. He scanned the area, looking for lingering hostiles, before he swung off the roan. After checking Jacob, he felt for pulses of the women. None were alive, including Alacrity, whose body lay between Rebecca and Mabel's.

"Utes," Tooonug said, getting to the wagon, and bringing with him the four horses.

"Utes killed them?" Cossette asked.

"Jacob killed the women," Stryker said.

Tooonug nodded in agreement. "It best. Utes very cruel." The Paiute adjusted the ropes in his hands.

"What do you mean?" Cossette asked.

"White squaw woman, Utes take, suffer much. Cut off ears, burn nose off with fire sticks up nose, cut baby out belly, kick til die. She watch. Then blind squaw eyes with fire sticks. Lead squaw around village with insides. Use insides like rope." Tooonug motioned as if he pulled out the intestines from his own stomach. "She happy she die on fire pole."

Cossette looked at Stryker, fear showing on her face.

"I won't let them jam burning sticks up your nose, or your ass. I'll shoot you first," Stryker said. He started back to the trail before she could say whether or not she felt comforted.

"Stryker! Wait!" Cossette yelled.

CHAPTER TWELVE

"We'll make early camp and ride past Orderville tonight," Stryker said, when the two caught up to him.

"Don't you want to tell them about the wagon?" Cossette asked, riding beside Stryker. She kept her eyes on the trail in front, and then suddenly looked around as if she forgot to be watchful. "And what about those Indians, wouldn't it be safer in town?"

"No fire tonight. We pass town after midnight. There's some grade after that. We'll rest at the top and push on."

"Tooonug, will they come after us, the Utes I mean," Cossette asked.

"They want horses. White woman." He paused, and then added. "Tracks not come this way now. Go up in mountain. Hide two, three days. Kill ox and eat."

"How many do you think there are?" She tried to ask casually.

"Tracks, arrows show seven, eight. They have gun now."

"How do you know?"

"White man who shoot women no have gun." Tooonug saw Cossette's worried brow. "Your man good with gun. He shoot you."

"I want one of those shotguns behind you, Tooonug," Cossette said, sounding more determined. "I want Stryker using the rifle and pistol both." She struggled to keep her lips from trembling.

That night they set up camp a short distance south of Orderville, nearly within shouting distance. Moving off the trail to be near the stream, they watered the horses and allowed them to graze on stem grass growing by the water. The horses remained saddled and no fire was lit. Tooonug threw his blanket on the ground closer to Stryker and Cossette's bedding than he had the previous night. The men arranged all the guns within easy reach. Cossette nestled tightly against Stryker under their blanket, her motive other than to keep warm. Tooonug sat with his cover draped around his shoulders. He did not sleep.

Stryker slept fitfully, as he always did, dozing off and on. After about twenty minutes, the woman beside him drifted into steady breathing and faintly snored. Dreams came often to the man. He seldom obtained deep restful sleep where dreams were absent. The visions visiting him never included those who met death from his bullets or blades. Their demise seldom evoked regret on his part. They placed their lives in jeopardy when they crossed him, not unlike an unwelcome cockroach in the kitchen. Others, bad luck on their part. One in particular, seeming like a hundred years ago, a different time, a different place still haunted his nocturnal slumber. No matter where he went during the day, she would find him at night, maybe because he wanted her to. But his wife's body was always mangled and her face always bloody.

"Aa-hhh!" Stryker woke himself.

"Where are they?" Cossette screamed. "Stryker, I can't see them." She whispered in his ear, reaching for the shotgun behind her.

Tooonug threw off the blanket. He raked the barrel of his shotgun back and forth, searching for movement in the shadows.

Stryker jerked upright. "We need to go. Get up." He got to his feet and took off to check the roan and Cossette's mount.

Tooonug gathered his blanket to follow but Cossette stopped him. "Why are we not stopping in Orderville?"

"Your man in big hurry. People have many questions about wagon killing. Take much time. And . . ." Tooonug saw Stryker returning.

"And what?" She asked.

Tooonug looked at Cossette and lowered his voice. "He know they take horses." He thumped a fist against his chest, indicating he meant his horses.

They remained close to the creek and skirted Orderville that night. The town itself was positioned almost a half-mile away on higher ground to avoid the occasional spring floods. Stryker's recollection of the long grade north of town proved accurate and they rested the horses after laboring uphill well past noon of the next day. Nearing six-thousand feet in elevation, the horses needed extra rest.

"Tooonug, why did you come way down here, away from your tribe, I mean," Cossette asked. The three of them sat on a grass covered knoll, in a wide, lush meadow, watching the horses graze.

"Utes take wife. I follow."

"You find her?"

"She dead. Chenoa run self on broke tree limb. She still live when Tooonug find her. Utes gone."

Cossette stared at the Paiute. For the briefest of moments his eyes showed a tinge of sadness. Then his face hardened. "Utes will die."

Cossette saw Stryker stop scanning their surroundings and suddenly look at the Paiute. He said nothing and got quickly to his feet. "Let's round up the horses and get on the trail."

The trail inclined gradually. They'd gained another five-hundred feet in elevation prior to stopping for an early camp. The red rock walls gave way to tree covered foothills with much taller mountains rising up behind them. In places the grassy valley narrowed to less than a hundred paces wide where the creek ran swiftly alongside the trail. On other sections of the trail, the meadow widened out a quarter mile before slanting up to Ponderosa pines on the slopes. Mule deer, pronghorn antelope, and wild turkeys seemed plentiful. They passed several in the wider meadows. Overhead, golden eagles and black tail hawks sailed a hundred feet above the ground seeking to make meals of rabbits or young whistle pigs. Stryker led his companions away from the meadow and up a game trail that ran beside a draw. There they made camp, sheltered by pines on the slopes collaring the draw. They had a clear view of the meadow. Holly bushes and fledging pines grew in the wash and it appeared many years had passed since water had coursed through the channel. Stryker figured it would take one hell of a downpour for water to flood the draw and the fading sky looked clear.

He built a small cooking fire at a bend in the draw, out of sight from the trail and meadow. When Cossette saw Stryker bring out salted pork and beans from his saddle bag, she came over. "Tend to the horses, I'll do this. Your cooking tastes like . . . how do I say in English? Shit." She exaggerated her French accent.

The stew was indeed tastier, and Stryker grunted his approval. Cossette accepted this effusive praise, and in a monotone said, "Monsieur, you mustn't go on so."

There wasn't much one could do with his meager provisions. Cossette tenderized the pork and pulled the beans from the fire at just the right moment. It made a difference. She offered food to Tooonug, but he declined, preferring instead his own dried berry stew. The improved chow for Stryker and Cossette and the clear night, made for a better night's rest.

The next morning after breakfast, Stryker was loading up the horses, as Tooonug walked down the draw to survey the meadow. He came back running. "Utes come!" Tooonug yelled as he ran. The Paiute grabbed a shotgun from his skittish horse.

"They see you?" Stryker shouted back, his voice much lower than the Paiute's."

"Tooonug . . ."

Suddenly the rest of the horses bolted up the draw. Six Utes charged down from the trees, yelling and whooping, four of them stringing and flinging arrows as they ran. Two knelt to aim repeaters but they caught a blast from Tooonug's shotgun. One was killed outright with most of his throat blown away. The other kneeling Ute took pellets in his eyes and face.

The remaining four came on, leaping bushes as they ran, and now swinging axes and knives, weapons garnered from whites.

Stryker barely had time to throw Cossette to the ground behind a shrub pine and pull the Peacemaker. He fired in rapid succession. A .44 slug smacked the chest of the lead Ute, killing him. A second round drilled into the belly of another. But it took three more shots to stop his charge.

Tooonug came attacking from the left, whirling, and slashing with the knife. He buried his blade in a Ute's armpit. The warrior dropped his arm and desperately tried to pull out the knife with his free hand. But, the blade held firm and he went to his knees, and then on his back, still pulling on the knife. Tooonug jumped on him. He straddled the Ute's chest and choked him with pent-up ferocity. Even though the wounded attacker fought desperately for his life, maniacally tugging at the hands around his throat, he couldn't dislodge the iron grip of a man so possessed. Veins in the Ute's face swelled as if ready to burst. His eyes bulged as Tooonug crushed his windpipe. Then, the Paiute continued choking a dead man.

The last Ute veered off, silent now save for his footfalls. He ran down the wash, dodging rocks and bushes as he headed toward the meadow. With one bullet left in the Colt, Stryker held fire. He flipped the gun into his left hand and tore at the cartridges in his belt.

At the end of the draw eight more Utes appeared. Seeing Tooonug fighting on the ground and Stryker furiously attempting to re-load, they charged.

Stryker jumped behind Cossette, giving up on extracting bullets from the tight leather loops. He yanked her up on her knees by the hair. She screamed in sudden pain. Stryker reached in his back pocket, and lifting her chin with the Colt's barrel, dug the razor point into Cossette's neck.

A rivulet of blood streamed down from the cut as Cossette struggled to protest through clenched teeth. "Help . . . me." The words bubbled in spittle. She squirmed mightily but Stryker held firm.

The Utes got to within thirty yards. Stryker stretched Cossette's neck up and back, jamming her head hard against his chest.

But the Utes faltered. A volley of arrows suddenly appeared in their chests. Within seconds, another wave of arrows rained down on the attackers. A chorus of war cries rang out behind Stryker and Cossette. He turned to see thirty or more Paiutes pouring down the draw, dashing by them, their knives and spears brandished, with bows now slung across their backs. Two broke off to pick up the repeater rifles of Utes felled by Tooonug's shotgun blast. Another Paiute ran up to scalp the two warriors, one who'd been blinded by pellets still living.

Five Utes went down from the two volleys of Paiute arrows. Those on the ground were dead or dying. Being the fastest warriors, they were in front when the arrows hit them. The three still standing in the rear turned to flee. But now their lack of speed failed them because the Paiutes quickly ran them down and the tribal anger at the Utes for wife stealing was borne in the ferociousness of the Paiute attack. Even though some among the Paiutes may have wanted to keep the Utes alive to torture, the others wrath prevailed, and they stabbed and bludgeoned them to death in a few short minutes.

Tooonug finally extracted his knife out of the dead Ute's armpit and ran to where the five Utes with arrows in them lay on the ground. He and another Paiute began the scalping. Tooonug chose two Utes who still clung to life. He knelt behind each one and lifted the shoulders. Putting a bracing knee between shoulder blades, he held up the head with a fistful of hair and ran his blade front to back. He stood over them staring down as they groaned. Then, as if suddenly aware of the horses, he sprinted up the draw to locate them.

Stryker withdrew the razor from Cossette's neck and dropped the Colt from her chin. She still bled, but not in spurts. She clapped her hand to her neck and pulled it away dripping in blood. She leaped to her feet. "Aahhh! Am I gonna bleed to death?" She urgently pressed her palm against the wound, her eyes terrified.

A Piute, standing on the edge of the wash, knelt and plucked a fistful of yarrow plant. He folded it into a thick ball and side-stepped down the dirt bank. The brave pulled Cossette's bloodied hand from her neck and pushed the herb on the cut. He then brought her hand back up to hold the yarrow in place. Offering only a slight nod of his head, he went off to join the braves rummaging through the belongings of the dead Utes.

Tooonug re-appeared, leading his horses from out of the trees and down the draw. "Not go far. Rope go round tree. Stop horse." He made a circular movement with his hand.

Jabbering excitedly and inspecting the horses, several of the Paiutes gathered around Tooonug. He accepted their praise and adulation by stretching his short frame to its full height and looking stoic.

113

It took Stryker longer to find the roan and Cosstte's mount. Both horses had galloped into the trees and stopped. Then finding themselves on a game trail, they followed it as it wound around a sloping ridge and down to the meadow. Stryker found them leisurely munching grass by the stream. Cossette and the Paiute warriors had already filed out of the draw. They met him halfway across the meadow.

The trail ran north along the west side of the meadow where it hugged the pine thickened hillside. Then, it coiled westerly up a grade through the trees. That's where Stryker saw the lead members of the Paiute tribe moving down the hill. Tutzegubet rode in front, a warrior riding a pony on each side of him. Behind them came a riderless horse, led by a brave on foot. That horse pulled a travois sled upon which rode the chief's rocking chair. Stryker couldn't see the rest of the tribe; however, those he saw had only three more horses and none of them with riders. They dragged sleds instead, and several dogs also pulled smaller versions of the travois. Women and some of the older children carried heavily burdened baskets.

Stryker figured the Paiute braves with him and Cossette, and Tooonug, were scouts, or more likely a hunting party, which just happened to come upon the Ute attack. They must have cut across the hill looking for game and had swung down the draw, toward the meadow, just in time to see the Utes attacking the three of them.

"What happened to my bullet?" Cossette asked.

She and Stryker rode alone. Tooonug had paid them no mind as they rode past him still receiving adulation from his fellow Paiutes. They soon passed by the migrating Paiutes and Cossette decided to ask Stryker about her nearly getting her throat slit.

"Had one left."

"So you intended to cut my throat and shoot yourself? I'd rather you use the gun on me! God! I can't believe . . . !" Cossette rubbed the front of her neck, as if to make sure Stryker's razor hadn't cut too deeply.

"You didn't have that choice, I did," Stryker said, without any hint of concern for the woman's view of matters. He scanned the landscape ahead. "We're probably two days ride to Panguitch. We should find a room or two to sleep there. Then get your ass ready for seven to ten days in the saddle. Send a telegram if you can."

"A bath and clean clothes; I must look a bloody mess. Two rooms," Cossette repeated thoughtfully. She *was* married; she reminded herself, and the Mormons? They wouldn't let a room to them if they knew Stryker wasn't her husband, although, they wouldn't have to know. Still, all things considered, she felt a little reluctant to cozy up to a man who'd dug a razor into her neck and had come within a hair's breadth of running it across her throat. And, it seemed as if hers wasn't the first neck he'd used that razor on. She thought of gagging on her own blood, dying, but not before those last hideous moments of life. A shudder coursed through her. "Yes, two rooms."

They rode into Panguitch, a Mormon settlement of about four hundred, by mid-afternoon of the second day. They ate a huge meal prepared by a plump hostess and got a much needed night's rest. The following morning Cossette made a show of procuring two more blankets prior to getting back on the trail. She'd decided they should continue sleeping separately. The implacable man riding beside her didn't seem to care anyway.

The days of hard riding grew wearisome, and by the fourth, talk shared between man and woman was restricted to sparse exchanges, and only when necessary. Each understood that ahead of them lay violent confrontations with the kidnappers in San Francisco. For Cossette, finding her husband and Montel could easily end poorly. She had more to worry about and it was she who cut back conversation the most. Stryker never started many conversations anyway. Regardless, there was no use hashing out what might happen. Cossette was wise enough to know Stryker didn't care who died, as long as he got what he wanted.

At one point on the trail, Cossette ventured past the cold pale eyes which were boring into hers, and said, "my butt is so sore, I'm gonna soak it in a hot tub for a week. And I'm never leaving San Francisco again, certainly not out to this uncivilized, God-forsaken country." She stood in the stirrups, like a circus rider.

Stryker let his eyes drift away from the woman, to survey the land around them. Several minutes passed, as he admired the vast landscape. "I figure it's that filthy city of misfits and assholes God shits on."

After that exchange, Cossette realized it would be useless to point out, what she believed, were the finer things about city culture. She eased her tortured rear back down on the saddle.

In Ogden they sold Cossette's horse to a young Mormon couple. Cossette thought the boy handsome and she insisted they practically give it to them. Stryker booked passage for him and Cossette on the train to San Francisco and arranged for the sometimes loyal roan's transit as well. They used the six hours prior to departure to bathe and change into clean clothes. Cossette bought an ankle-length woolen dress, and a long coat. Stryker dug out a clean shirt from his saddlebag.

Stryker stretched his long legs under the seat in front of him and dozed most of the trip to Reno. Cossette, who sat by the window, leaned against it, making up for many, near sleepless nights, on cold hard ground. It wasn't until after the train completed the long arduous climb from Reno to the Sierra's crest, that Stryker broke out of an extended, awkward silence.

"Where did you last see Montel or your husband?" Stryker asked, from under a lowered hat brim.

Cossette glanced at Stryker before she answered. "Montel and his brutes, Jack and Shorty, broke into our apartment. I left them there. And I don't know where they took him. His back . . ."

"I'll go there first," Stryker interrupted.

"Good, it's south of the Golden Gate Park, in a deplorable ten-by-ten rat hole on the second floor. The rats don't mind the stairs. I'll take you to it."

"More than one door?"

"No, the outside stairs climb up from the alleyway, only way in or out." Cossette shifted to peer out the window. Perhaps she wasn't really looking at the spectacular scenery, because she turned back to Stryker and said, "I play the violin. I play it most well."

It took a few moments. Stryker remained motionless for several long minutes while Cossette waited for his response. He wondered if she were attempting to imply that skills she demonstrated in her own environment somehow made up for her lack of skill in his. She would have no way of knowing he did indeed appreciate good music. Leigh had insisted they attend the symphony and he begrudgingly went. At first he hated it because the songs sounded like notes which had been dumped into a bucket and then poured out on a hard floor. To him, the music bounced around, jumbled with no fluidity. And, it often came out repetitious and sounding angry. Maybe he was no judge of music. So what, he wasn't about to pretend. Then, he finally heard pieces he enjoyed, *Moonlight Sonata, Fur Elise,* and lately, one of the prostitutes in Virginia City played a *Gymnopedie* piece on the piano he liked very much. The girl said she got it from some Frenchman when she "worked" in Paris. The music was sad, and afterwards, he fucked her sadly.

He raised a tanned forefinger, tipped the hat back. "Play for me sometime."

Cossette, tired of waiting for a response, had let the Sierras recapture her attention. His request startled her. She turned back to him, a quizzical expression on her cocked head. "You? It's not a fiddle. It's a violin. They're different."

The hat got lowered again. "Don't like fiddling."

She opened her mouth to say something more, but the Stetson's repositioning stopped the words in her throat, about where the razor would have cut.

After that exchange with the exception of perfunctory comments during train stops, not much else passed between the two. Cossette's worry about her husband grew with each passing mile and Stryker ran potential courses of action through his brain. He was schooled as a teenager on a gun crew in the Civil War, and later, he learned from the Sioux, the Apache, Comanche, and the Ute, fighting in the Indian campaigns. The classes were brutal. The only passing grade given out was survival. Shocking vile acts of torture he eventually came to admire, because they achieved results, efficiently. Repulsive at first, then mind-numbing inuring to the savagery, and finally, perhaps inevitably, Stryker recognized their effectiveness . . . their usefulness. A man willing to bring these "skills" to a civilized society would find them useful against hardened criminals. He was through fucking around with Montel.

"I sent Montel a telegram asking where to find Claude, to please reply at the Oakland office," Cossette announced, as the train pulled out from Sacramento. "Do you think he'll be all right, Stryker? I hope I find out in Oakland."

"Hope's never worked for me, and when we get to Oakland, we separate."

"They'll be there?"

"You told them when and where to find you. I'll be around, but from now on, you're on your own. Write your address on the ticket." Stryker dug out the ticket and a pencil from his shirt pocket. He paused while she scribbled down her address. "Go to the Palace Hotel and stay there. See Senator Hearst. He's at the hotel. Tell him what you know and wait for me." Stryker rose and found a seat next to a scruffy old man in the back of the coach. He stretched out his legs and pulled the brim of his hat down.

With that, Cossette sat alone on the train. Suddenly, she thought about the prospect of living alone. Even out on the run she felt as if she did have companionship. The Mormons for the most part were friendly and helpful. This man Stryker, although his edges were jagged and he almost killed her, did afford her protection. The realization momentarily struck her; if he hadn't needed her to find Montel, he most likely would have killed her. After all, it was a nasty trick to play on him, she thought. But her loyalty to her husband outweighed all. She wondered if the man who sat in the back of the coach thought about that.

It had grown dark outside the window. Rain began to speckle the glass. Instead of seeing the landscape floating by, she saw the outline of her own reflection staring back at her. A lone face looked at the window, no one else in the glass, not Claude, or Stryker, just her. It had been a long tortuous trip from Montreal to New Orleans, and then to San Francisco. Without Claude by her side, she doubted she would have made it. Now if he were gone, dead, what would she do? A woman alone had few choices to make a living out west, none too appealing.

And she got no telegram when she got to Oakland.

By the time they transferred from the train to the ferry, it was early evening, and they pulled away from Oakland at six-thirty. Cossette sat on a seat inside, away from the cold, drizzling rain. The mixed-breed remained outside, standing at the rail. The bay water was choppy and waves sloshed against the bow. Night arrived early because of the rain and he could see lights from San Francisco about fifteen minutes out of Oakland. Here, he was coming back with no signature and no Montel. Fooled by a woman . . . and he'd protected her afterwards. Damn, he felt like an idiot. He'd failed Hearst. Sorry Senator, you hired a fool. Morgan was under one of those lights in the distance and he wasn't exactly riding back to her in triumph. Shit, let her down too. He'd had his share of mistakes in his thirty-some years. Men had lost their lives. It happens in battle. But he had never felt as bad as he did tonight in the rain.

CHAPTER THIRTEEN

"It's been five and a half weeks." George Hearst stood peering out the window in his suite at the Palace. "I fear the man will chase Montel all over the West and still not catch him. I knew that damn Frenchman would be slippery and now that we realize political motivation is behind his recalcitrance, I can see there is more than one chain securing the *Examiner*. Others, who likewise bend in the wind chasing Montel's socialist utopia, have also wrapped fetters around the paper. Each one has to be pried loose. This is more difficult than I first thought." He turned away from his reflective musing in the glass and said to the straight-backed woman standing in the middle of the room, "Morgan, can we win this fight?"

"Yes, because we have to."

A hint of a smile crept to one corner of his mouth. "I'd trusted you'd say that." He squared his shoulders to face her. "Have you heard from Stryker? The last I heard he was leaving Virginia City."

"No."

"He may need help. I can't give him any, though. He was brought in, as you know, because I have to keep the paper interests from the public. If not for William, I'd just let it go. Anyway, Stryker will have to do this on his own." The Senator hesitated, soliciting comment.

"You're right and I don't know why we haven't heard from him. He knows we'll want to be kept aware . . ." Morgan stopped in mid-sentence, abruptly considering there could be an unpleasant reason for Stryker's lack of contact. Another, more acceptable reason could be he had no progress to report and simply chose not to relay it. Whatever the reason, it would serve no purpose to speculate or react emotionally. "Until I learn differently, I'll think Stryker is still out there hunting down Montel, and he will get him."

"Me too." Hearst forced a smile.

In another part of the city, Montel had made the decision to tell Barry Blankton of his plans. "I've received a telegram. The assassin sent to kill me has himself been killed by hostiles. Since the sender of the telegram is due to arrive back here soon, and I've heard nothing more about the man, I've good reason to believe it's true."

"Wonderful news, if true. What's the reasoning?" Blankton asked, not sounding too convinced.

"The Frenchman I sent in my place is coming home, alone." Montel slyly left out Cossette being the decoy. He accurately surmised Blankton would be even more suspicious if he knew the person sent out to lead Stryker on a deceptive quest was a woman. "That man is traveling alone, and conspicuous, and unafraid."

"That's what he told you?"

"I had one of my own men take the Oakland ferry to follow him. He stopped at the telegraph office like he said he would. My man saw him do that and then he boarded the ferry alone. No one else even spoke to him."

"I got you out of that stinking apartment, put you up on the top floor of the Palace, and gave you Webster, one of my most trusted men, so you wouldn't use your Asian, all so you'd keep the paper. By the way, where does that "Chink"-Li think you are?"

"Chang-Li, thinks like everybody else, that I left the city. Unless you told someone else. . ." Montel started to say.

"No! No, no one knows, just you, me, and Webster. And Web won't talk. Besides, he knows I'll have him killed. He knows Vance didn't kill himself." Blankton chuckled.

"I'm so tired of being cooped up in this damn room." Montel drew a deep breath and blew it out in a loud huff.

"This 'damn' room is a suite, and a damn nice one. Old man Hearst would bust a hemorrhoid if he knew you were on the same floor and just around the corner . . . and in a suite just like his." Blankton chortled again. "It wasn't easy getting you up here, even in the middle of the night. Can't take a chance you stepping outside that door, we've waited this long."

"Worth it, I guess. If he hadn't wanted the *Examiner* for his kid, we could've outlasted him. His health is going. I coulda just run the paper 'til he died off, no one the wiser." Montel plopped himself into a cushioned chair.

"Remember Alain, this is not just about you or us. This is about our great cause. We have to do whatever it takes . . . whatever it takes. What about that French couple?" Blankton faced Montel directly. "They'll have to be silenced, you know."

"The husband will be taken care of, and the wife—well, we'll get to her. First I want to find out for sure if that man Hearst brought in is dead."

"Has anyone seen this fellow, know anything about him? Who is he?"

"Only Winslow and he got the shit beat out of him by the man. Winslow thinks I've left San Francisco too, so I haven't talked with him myself, just heard second hand. The man's called Stryker. A wrangler of sorts I guess, but a tough one. Sent two men to deal with him. He slit one's throat and I haven't heard from the other."

"But he's dead." Blankton said, in a tone that begged for confirmation.

"That's what I want to make sure of. That is, before we take care of the husband. I'll get a report soon, got a couple of my boys waiting for him where he and his wife live. They'll get the truth out of her," Montel asserted with assurance.

"Her?"

"Huh?'

You said you'd get the truth outta *her.*"

"Oh, yeah I meant him, the husband."

A knock at the door interrupted them. The door opened before either could react and Webster entered with two dinner trays.

"Thanks, Webster, that's all for now." Blankton waited for him to leave before continuing. "Alain, send your man over to where they live. Find out all you can from them. I want to know how the assassin died, where, and what Indians. In other words, I want proof. Have him report back here to you. And if this Stryker fellow is alive . . ."

"If he's alive, I'll send enough men to find him and kill 'im, wherever he is."

Stryker waited for Cossette to leave the ferry and he watched her enter the Ferry House before he ambled down the ramp next to a woman he didn't know. He walked through the building and stepped outside where he paid for the roan to be stabled. There he hailed a horse drawn cab to take him to the Affair's flat. He would have gone to see Winslow first but his gut told him to go to the apartment.

The cab traveled past the Palace Hotel and, for a brief moment, he thought about Morgan. Then he remembered Hearst and his mission, the mission he had failed to complete. "Driver, let me off four blocks before you get to the address."

It had started to drizzle and, as they climbed the hill district, they ran into mists near the crest. The streets were unpaved after leaving downtown proper and the horse's hooves made sucking sounds in the mud. The rain fell harder. Soon it got so dark, Stryker wondered how the driver could see where he was going. All the buildings were dwellings, rentals he figured. He saw no for sale signs, but did see plenty of rentals for lease. What buildings Stryker could see were almost all single-story, and dilapidated. Cossette lived in a shabby neighborhood.

"Whoa there," The driver pulled back on the reins. "Seventy-five cents. Your house is down a ways, might be a two-story, according to the number, I think."

Stryker paid the charge and nothing extra. The driver having gotten a good look at Stryker earlier wisely decided not to make the lack of a tip an issue.

The driver was right. It was a two-story. Stryker found it without much difficulty. The alleyway and stairs were on the left side of the building. He'd started to ascend the steps when the door above opened.

"What else you want besides whiskey?"

123

Stryker couldn't see the man in the doorway, but he heard him, even over the rain pounding on the roof.

"No, I ain't gettin' no sandwiches, Al. This shithole ain't fit to eat in."

Another man inside yelled something Stryker couldn't understand. "Ah, fuck you," the man at the door said. And, he slammed the door. "I'll get back 'fore she gets here asshole. It's only four blocks," he said, stomping down the steps, signaling his anger.

Stryker slipped back from the corner, pulled the Peacemaker, and waited. When he heard the man's boots come off the last board and onto dirt, he stepped around the corner. Stryker thumbed back the Colt's hammer. "What's your name?"

He'd been looking down, shielding his eyes from the rain, when Stryker asked his name. He couldn't hear the cocking of the pistol for the rain, but when he looked up, he saw Stryker with a gun pointed at his gut. The man, a head shorter than the mixed-breed and with a belly providing a big target for the Colt, stopped dead in his tracks.

"Mike." Mike wore a nine-inch knife stuck in his belt, right side, but no gun.

"Back up the stairs, Mike. Take off the boots first," Stryker ordered.

Mike backed up to the stairs and sat to pull the boots from his feet. He kept his eyes on the gun as he struggled to get his feet out of the boots. Finally, he got the second boot off and started to stand.

"Not yet. Throw the knife in the mud. Left hand."

Mike used his left hand to withdraw the big blade from the wide, leather belt and toss it on the ground.

"Who you talking to up there?"

"Al," Mike growled.

Stryker made two quick upward movements with the Colt's barrel for Mike to stand. Mike rose, turned, and started up the stairs in his stocking feet. Stryker followed. Near the top of the stairs, Stryker eased the hammer forward. Mike turned the door knob and Stryker laid the butt of the Peacemaker against the side of his head with enough force to drop him to his knees. Another blow to his head and Mike fell through the door, unconscious.

Al, who'd been sitting by a table in the center of the apartment, jumped to his feet and eyed the holster hanging from a peg on the wall next to Stryker, where he'd hung his rain jacket, his hat, and his gun. He decided to sit back down.

Stryker took the pistol from the wall and tossed it over his shoulder. The gun hit the street and half-buried itself in mud below. The stench of putrefied flesh inside the room overwhelmed him. It not only pervaded the nostrils, it coated the tongue. If Stryker had not often experienced the smell of rotting flesh in war, he would have vomited.

Two lanterns lit the twelve-by twelve foot room, one on the wall by the door and one on the table. The walls were as bare as the floor, both clean, but both bare. There was a small window in the kitchen area to Stryker's left but even when the sun shone it provided little light, and the sun wasn't shining. On Stryker's right, a bed had been shoved against the wall. On it, a man lay face down, hands and feet lashed to the frame. Stryker figured him to be Claude, Cossette's husband. The flickering lantern still cast enough light, showing a hideously disfigured face and bloodied hands and feet. The nose and lips were missing; just crimson vestiges of the facial features in their place. A jaw had a fist size hole in it. Several fingers and toes were bloody stubs with whitish bones protruding out the stump ends.

Stryker sidestepped to the bed. With his free hand he felt Claude's throat. He lived. Stryker placed the Colt's barrel against the back of Claude's head and pulled the trigger.

Al warily watched Stryker step across the floor to where Mike lay on his side. The mixed-breed shifted the gun to his left hand and withdrew the straight razor from his back pocket. He kicked Mike onto his back and knelt beside him. With a surgeon's proficiency, he dug the point of the razor into an eye socket and sliced in behind the eye. He then used the bridge of Mike's nose as a fulcrum and popped out the eyeball. It landed on the floor, and the eye wobbled crazily on the wooden plank. He did the same to the other eye. Stryker straightened. The eyes had fallen on each side of Mike's head and Stryker used his boot to step on them, squashing each one like a grape.

Al sat mortified, staring at Mike's empty eye sockets. Blood drained in crimson rivulets down each side of his face, quickly turning black with oxygen exposure. In the dull lantern light, it all looked black to Al.

Finally Al mustered enough courage to ask, "Mister, what you want?"

"Montel."

"If I tell you, you'll leave? I mean and not . . .?"

"You're gonna die. Up to you how." Stryker cut in.

"He was like that when we came here," Al said, looking fearfully at Claude's corpse. Other men, they're here 'fore us. They tied him up, left him like that. I killed two rats here this morning!" Al's voice rose in growing desperation.

Stryker stepped over Mike, who'd had begun to groan, shifted the razor, and moved around the table toward Al. "Where is he?"

"Oh God! I . . ."

Stryker fired the Colt. The .44 bullet tore into Al's left kneecap, shattering it, and blasting through the joint to shred bone and tissue onto the floor underneath. Stryker thumbed the hammer back again.

"The Palace Hotel! He's at the Palace Hotel!" Al grabbed at his leg above the knee with his hands. "Please mister, I've got a wife, three kids. I ain't done nothing like this. I'm just here. Please . . ."

Stryker leveled the Peacemaker and sent another slug into Al's face. The bullet entered his upper lip and burrowed through his mouth and throat. Miraculously, Al still lived. He brought both hands to his face, and then struggled to hold them there as blood poured from his mouth. His hands fell away, he slumped forward, and his face hit the table with a loud thud.

Stryker smashed the lantern with the gun barrel. Kerosene splashed onto the table and over the mortally wounded Al. The spilt lamp oil ignited, engulfing Al's head and shoulders, who, still clinging to life, groaned in a new pain.

Stryker holstered the Colt and shifted the razor to his right hand. He walked over to where Mike lay and started to kneel. Changing his mind, he shoved the razor back in his pocket and stepped over Mike, reaching for the kitchen lamp. He opened the door and went outside before tossing the lamp at Mike's head, closing the door when the flames jumped to life on Mike's torso. Mike apparently regained consciousness long enough to feel the fire; he screamed twice. After that he didn't scream anymore.

Outside, Stryker headed down the stairs. Water poured so heavily from the sky one would wonder how it got up in the air in the first place. It pounded the tin roofs with such force it may have masked the gunshots. The street appeared empty from what he could see through the rain, anyway. When he was about halfway down the stairs, a buggy appeared below him. A man wearing a long black coat and a broad brim hat stepped out. He glanced up and to see Stryker pull a gun and hurriedly jumped back into the buggy. Stryker couldn't see inside the buggy, but he saw the reins snap, heard a command shouted. The horse jumped forward, took off in a gallop, and the buggy quickly disappeared in the rain.

Stryker walked six blocks through the deluge before he encountered a cab. "The Palace Hotel" he told the driver.

So, all that time he'd been traipsing around Nevada and Utah, Montel was wallowing in luxury at the most fabulous hotel in the country. "That cocksucker!" In his mind, he heard Alacrity yell her last words to him. *"Hope you get that cocksucker!"* Shit, not yet, sweet cheeks. He wiped the rain from his scraggily beard and spit.

Another rain drenched buggy was inside the hotel carriage entrance, with the horse's sides heaving and its nostrils blowing steam. The buggy was empty, no driver, and not a cab. An negro attendant stood by the horse, preparing to lead it away. "Who owns this buggy?" Stryker asked him.

"Don't know his name, suh. He come here a lot past month or two."

"He wore a long black coat tonight?"

"Yes suh, he was."

"Know where he went?"

"No suh, but he usually go all way to the top, takes that rising room over there," the attendant said, pointing. He dropped his arm, took hold of the bridle, and started walking away.

Stryker headed toward the rising room while glancing up at the seventh floor. It had taken him at least fifteen minutes to flag down a cab and he would be lagging that much behind the black coat. The man wearing it could be anywhere in the hotel, or even outside it. After taking a quick look in the bar and parlor room, Stryker continued on, quickening his long strides to the lift. He stepped aboard and asked the uniformed operator. "You take a fellow wearing a long black overcoat up in the last few minutes?"

The sixty-something fellow eyed Stryker carefully, taking in the countenance of the man, and answered, "I did."

"Seventh floor?"

"That's right."

"See where he went?"

"No, I did not." The operator seemed visibly relieved he could provide no more information. When Stryker stepped from the platform into the hallway of the seventh floor without offering a thank you, the staff member said, "you're welcome" to himself. If Stryker heard him, he ignored the sarcasm.

"You saw him?" Montel asked, after Webster had taken off his overcoat and vigorously shaken off the rainwater, much to the annoyance of the Frenchman. He appeared visibly shaken. Not only was the man not dead, he was here, in San Francisco!

"I saw him coming down the stairs at their apartment. Raining hard, but I could see well enough to tell he sure fit Winslow's description of him."

"And you came straight here?"

"I tore outta there, sure. I went south first, 'cause that's the way I parked the buggy, then I turned around by cutting over a street. Came straight here after that to tell you."

"You fool. He could have followed you!"

"I didn't see no horse!" Webster blurted back, bordering on a whine.

"You tell anybody, I mean anybody! That I'm here?"

"No." Webster could have sounded surer.

Montel picked up on it. "You tell anybody *you* were staying here?"

"I might've tolt Mike or Al . . . but I never, ever mentioned your name. I tolt 'em, I thought you left town, just like you said." Webster emphasized the last part, sounding more believable.

"I told you what I'd do if you blabbed dammit!"

"I didn't tell 'em! I swear to God!"

A Remington derringer appeared in Montel's hand so quickly Webster failed to see where it came from. The pop it made when fired belied its deadly effectiveness and the .41 slug plowed deep into Webster's chest. An expression appeared on his face as if he couldn't comprehend Montel had just shot him. His mouth gaped open in protest but he could muster only a gagging sound from the back of his throat.

"Should have sworn to me. I'm the one with the gun," Montel said.

Webster staggered a short step and collapsed to his knees. His eyes stared ahead blankly, unable now to see Montel. The inescapable realization that his life would last but a few more moments, engulfed him–a few precious seconds of being *someone*, of being *Webster Dodd Wilkens*. He never really thought about death, about how he would die, nor did he think of it now. He just thought about how *he* was coming to a close and yet, as he did, he knew he'd never felt so alive. Putting life right up next to death, as opposites, made living starkly clear. Then his ability to think drained away. He fell forward, his chest and face hit the floor first, and he lay on the floor dead.

Montel stepped around Webster's body and ran to the door. He swept up his coat from the chair there and gripped the doorknob. Then he released the knob and spun around. His eyes darted around the room, searching for objects which suggested he, and not Webster, was the room's guest. He'd been careful. What clothing and personal items he had in the room could easily be Webster's. Papers, documents, got burned. He smiled inwardly as he dashed over to the window.

Rain cascaded down outside like a waterfall, and when he raised the glass, he got drenched. He held the window's bottom sash up and he slid a leg over the sill. Searching with his foot, he found the balcony flooring and he slipped the other leg out. He remained facing the room, his back to the rain, and eased the window down. Shielding his eyes with one hand as a visor, he clung to building's lattice work with the other, and moved along the narrow balcony to the short banister. He stepped over that and out onto a cement ledge. Using the perilous footing on the ledge, he managed to shuffle his feet to another balcony where he rested and ruefully thought he should have rushed out the door and taken his chances on being seen. He repeated the terrifying feat four more times. Each time he passed a window he did so with the additional fear of being seen, but that didn't happen. The rooms were lit; however, he was so focused on not falling, he never looked to see if they were occupied. Montel fought off the nearly insane urge to simply push away from the wall and fling himself out midair by shutting his eyes and focusing on gripping his fingers to handholds on the architectural design features. The driving rain pounded his back and pressed him to the wall. Finally, he came to the room he figured to be across from the fire escape door, and fortunately, the room was dark. His fingers fought frantically to find enough grip to raise the wet window.

Stryker had gone past two doors in the hallway when he heard what sounded like a loud Champaign cork pop. Only Champaign pops weren't that loud. He began turning doorknobs. Three doors had been left unlocked and he made inglorious entrances into each room. The first one had two elderly women getting ready for bed. In the second, a man was dining alone, and the third room had an older gentleman being "entertained" by a much younger woman. He sat on the side of the bed wearing, an undershirt, boxer-type shorts, and sock suspenders holding up his black socks. The young lady knelt in front of him. Neither noticed the mixed-breed who entered and left quietly. A fourth unlocked door swung open and revealed a prone man bleeding on the floor, a black coat next to him. Stryker rolled him over to discover he had no breath in him. Instead, he had a bullet in his chest.

A small stream of blood ran from the corner of the man's mouth and pooled beneath his cheek on the carpet. His lifeless eyes failed to properly greet Stryker.

"If Montel was here, he wasn't too happy to see you," Stryker growled to the dead man. He rose and surveyed the room. No sign of a struggle and the blood looked fresh. Stryker turned, thoughtfully studied the door for a few seconds, and then moved quickly to the window. Water on the sill, a damp carpet, and he figured a person wouldn't open the window for fresh air in a rain storm. He raised the sash and battled the driving rain pelting his face. Leaning out as far as he could he looked right, then left. There, he saw the shadow of a figure a few rooms away, struggling to open a window.

Montel had his eyes screwed shut, attempting to let his fingers feel for a handhold. Then, much to his relief, the window began rising. Lowering his head and grunting, he pulled with all his strength, to lift the window higher. Suddenly, a hand grabbed the front of his coat and, with a hard jolt, ripped him out of the rain, and threw him to the floor inside.

The door opened behind Stryker. A plainclothes hotel guard, brandishing a twelve-gauge shotgun, and two armed policemen in dark blue uniforms wearing their derby hats, rushed into the room. The hotel lift operator followed. "He the one asking about the deceased?" one of the policemen, a sergeant, asked, pointing his revolver at Stryker.

"Yes, that's him," the nervous staff member answered.

"He tried to kill me too!" Montel yelled, struggling to his feet behind Stryker. "If you hadn't stopped him, I'da been the second man he killed tonight."

"You're under arrest for murder, mister. Take his gun, Art. And don't get between him and the shotgun."

Stryker allowed the junior officer to slip the Peacemaker from his holster without protest. He did so out of consideration of Hearst and Morgan, as well as the shotgun.

"Who are you and whatcha doing outside that window?" The police sergeant gruffly asked Montel.

Montel made astute decisions. "Montel, I'm Alain Montel of the *San Francisco Examiner*, and I was walking down the hall, heard a shot, and this man burst out of a room." He thumbed at Stryker and scooted around him. "I started running and he chased me. I ran into this room. It was empty, unlocked." Montel hesitated, and then went on with his story. "I forgot to lock the door, like an idiot." Montel threw out his hands as if to gesture stupidity. "And, I came over there

131

to climb out the window." He dropped a hand and directed the other one toward the window. "He grabbed me just as you came in."

"What did you want with Mister Montel?" The sergeant, a big man who sported a barrel-sized beer belly, asked Stryker.

"Cut out his lying tongue," Stryker growled.

"He looks like he'd do it," the junior policeman, smaller in stature, offered. As he backed away from Stryker, he pointed both his service revolver and the Peacemaker at Stryker.

"Put them irons on him." The sergeant dug handcuffs from a black leather pouch he wore on his uniform belt, and handed them to Art who put Stryker's Colt in his belt to take the cuffs. He side-stepped wide around Stryker, and then inched up behind him. "You need to bring your hands behind you, mister."

But Stryker didn't move his hands.

"Look here tough man, you can come along to jail, or get carried to the mortuary," the sergeant growled.

Stryker's eyes narrowed to silver slits. He tightened his muscles, coiled them ready to spring. He'd given up the Peacemaker. Handcuffing asked too damn much.

The Sergeant turned his revolver slightly away from the mixed-breed, using two hands to cock the gun. He pointed it at Stryker's chest.

Stryker made his move, or rather started to make his move. The butt of Art's gun crashed into the side of his head first.

CHAPTER FOURTEEN

He woke up on a cot in a windowless eight by twelve cell, dark and cave like. The walls were brick and the door, a heavy black hulk of iron, had one small pass through window. Below that was a slit for a food tray, both closed. The jail was built to hold the most heinous criminals.

"Welcome to your new home." A voice, presumably from a man on another cot, so presumed because Stryker couldn't see him in the dark cell, extended the greeting.

"What is this place?" Stryker grimaced. His head throbbed on each word.

"Broadway Jail, it's on Broadway Street, clever of 'em, huh. What you in here for?" The mature voice suggested its owner had lots of rings around his trunk.

Stryker put his hand on a sizable knot growing on the back of his head and started to sit up. The effort aggravated the knot and he lay back down. "They think I killed a man."

"You murder him?"

"Not that one."

The fellow in the other cot paused, obviously considering whether or not to continue the conversation. He'd gotten a look at his new cell mate when they brought him through the door, and even though Stryker had come in on a stretcher, the old timer could tell the most recent guest was well over six feet. "I'm in this hell hole 'cuz they say I assaulted a woman. I'm innocent though, like you." He attempted to curry favor. "Name's Raymond, Ray is what most people call me. You got a name?"

"Shut up."

Stryker was in no mood to engage in conversation. Matters had gone from bad to shit--chasing the fake Montel over three states, finally getting his hands on the real one and having him slip away was bad enough. Now, he could hang for a murder Montel committed. He'd scraped the bottom of the barrel so hard that he fell through the damn thing and it seemed as if the only way out was at the end of a rope. "Hell," Stryker told himself, "I have to get out of this fucking jail just to get back up to the bottom of the barrel." Normally, Stryker allowed very little of such musings, wouldn't have answered the first of Ray's questions either, but the blow on his head jostled a brain accustomed to clear, straight line thinking. He had to concentrate, figure a way out of this mess. But the throbbing pain in his head made focusing difficult.

Alain Montel waited in the hallway until they'd carried Stryker to the lift before he slipped away to the fire-escape stairwell. He held on to the safety railing, taking the steps two at a time to reach the bottom and exit out to the alley. He started out running, slipped and fell hard on a wet sidewalk, and walked the rest of the way in the rain to reach Barry Blankton at the Savoy.

He found Blankton on the second floor. The owner's office had been expanded and richly carpeted with a maroon rug from Persia. Fine mahogany from Indonesia paneled the walls. He sat in an outsized executive chair behind an outsized desk with a near full bottle of Scotch on it. Alain rushed in unannounced. He was still breathing hard and blurted out he'd killed Webster and narrowly escaped from the man who'd been after him.

Blankton spun around from gazing out the window and watching rain fall, to face Montel. "Why did you kill him? Why the hell are you here?"

"I had no choice. If I'd left him there alive, he would have surely told what he knew to that man! He's a killer, you know. And he would have found out about me from Web before he killed him, I'm sure.

Besides you, no one else knows I'm in San Francisco!" Montel, wet, stressed, and exasperated, replied to Blankton's accusation of acting stupidly. "Actually," he continued less agitatedly. "I believe it'll turn out rather brilliantly. The police think he did it."

"They do?" Barry Blankton sounded incredulous. "They think he killed Webster? Why?" In his hand he spun an empty diamond-cut crystal Old-Fashioned glass with cursive initials *BB*, on it. He sat it on the desk with a loud thud. Before he enjoyed a drink so damnably interrupted, he wanted good news to wash down his throat along with the Scotch.

Montel allowed a small chuckle, watching Blankton settle down as well. He could now impress Barry with his own quick thinking. "The brute had me by my coat, looked like he was attacking me when the police broke into the room. I told them he ran out of my suite right after I heard the shot which killed Web. I said he came after me when he saw me, to kill the only witness. Ha, ha, they bought it. They didn't bother to search me." Montel sensed he was on solid ground. "And, I tell you that man even looked like the killer. I've never seen a meaner looking devil."

"Well, I hope you're right." Blankton cocked an eyebrow. "I wouldn't like the idea of you plugging me, *the only other man who knows your whereabouts* with that little pop gun."

"I need a place to stay, just to be sure he's convicted 'fore I show myself. He might somehow get out and he'll be--how you say in America--mighty pissed." He plopped down in one of two stuffed chairs in front of the desk. "I could use a glass of wine." Montel twisted around in the chair, searching for where a bottle might be stored.

"They'll need you for a witness, Alain." Blankton had lifted a freshly poured glass of Scotch from his desk and sipped from it. "You Frenchie's, can't handle a man's drink, have to drink your wine. In that cabinet." Blankton saluted the cabinet with his glass. "You get 'sh-faaaced', not shit-faced. "Say, what do the police have as a motive for the killing? Why'd they think he did it? Webster wasn't robbed, right?"

"No, I didn't rob him. Not sure, though, 'bout what the police think, I mean. But even if he tries to claim I killed Web, they won't believe him. And to them, I surely don't have a motive. That man looks the part of a hired killer. I don't. And that is why I want to hide out until I know for certain he can't get out. He scares me, scares the hell out me."

"Well, you can't hide under this desk."

"I don't want to leave town, can't go back to the Palace, can't go back to my house or that apartment. C'mon Barry, I need damn room!"

"You know Alain, I'm starting to think you might be better off dead." Blankton's laugh sounded a little hollow. His smile gone, he stared at Montel, menacingly.

"That's not funny, Barry. Besides, I don't know who'd get the paper. I don't have it in a will. I don't have a will."

"All right," Blankton said. The smile returned. He scooted his chair closer to the desk and drew out a pen and paper. He spoke as he wrote. "Take this to Roger down at the *Marcy*. It's docked for repairs at the Fisherman's west end, Gashouse Cove. Should be there a couple more months at least. Here," he said, as he folded and handed the paper to Montel. "Tell him no one's to know about you. You'll take one of the empty passenger cabins but you'll have to work so as to not draw attention to yourself. How are you at scrubbing decks?"

Stryker needed rest, time to clear his mind. He had no idea what time it was. It had taken until well after midnight to get the paperwork completed and anyway, with the dank cell as black as a coal mine, he couldn't tell if the sun were up or not. He lay on the side opposite the knot and shut his eyes. Within a few moments it seemed lighter with his eyes closed.

It was a bright summer morning in eastern Pennsylvania, the sun having peaked over one of the distant hills. Treeless hills, green with tall lush grass, rolled across a wide valley between two wooded ridges at least ten miles apart. He'd been walking a dirt path which snaked among the hills, coming from nowhere, going to nowhere. Lost maybe, he didn't have a purpose, didn't have a destination. He was just there. He seemed to float along the path. Up on top of the next hill a shadow, silhouetted in the rising sun, perhaps a person. He began to climb toward it. At first, he stepped up through the grass with ease. He lost sight of the figure but he knew it remained in place, waiting for him. The ascent grew steeper. He dropped to all fours, pulling with his hands clawing at the clumps of grass, his legs pushing, but aching as if flush with lactic acid. The hill grew steeper and steeper, until completely vertical. He hung onto the side, pulling himself up, until finally he swung one of his legs over the top edge. There, not more than a hundred feet away, the figure stood, waiting, watching him struggle on all fours. He felt exhausted, and yet he fought on. He crawled over a mound; the figure, only fifty feet away, stood on top of another small rise. Struggling to his feet, he stood. He let his legs carry him down the mound; his legs ached mightily with each jolting step. He got to the little rise where he could tell the figure was a woman waiting. The pain vanished. He could walk straight toward her with ease. She smiled. The sun sparkled through the ends of her blond hair. She was stunningly beautiful. He came closer. Although she smiled, tears flowed from blue eyes, from Leigh's blue eyes. Leigh! You're alive! He ran to hold her, to *be* with her again. After all the years, the long torturous years, the grieving, and the guilt of being partly responsible for her death, Leigh wasn't dead. She was here! On this hill! Alive!

But when he reached her she was gone. He looked around for her—nothing. In the back of his mind he knew it. He knew Leigh was dead. He knew it was just a dream. He knew it was a dream even before he woke up in the black jail cell.

"Ray, tell about the assault," he said, anything to get away from it.

"You talk in your sleep boy."

"Tell it."

Ray sat up on the edge of his cot. "Oh, all right. Me and Tony, we own a grocery on . . . doesn't matter where I guess. We sell fruit, vegetables, meats, and . . ." Ray heard a low groan from the other cot. "Okay, okay, day 'fore yesterday this middle-aged woman came up to me outside, we have fruits and vegetables on the sidewalk in baskets during the day. They bring 'em at night. She comes up and wants to buy a half a cantaloupe. We don't sell a half, for crying out loud. We sell 'em whole. Who the heck sells half a cantaloupe?"

Stryker began to wonder if they'd hang him twice for two murders.

"We argued for twenty minutes, me telling her no, her asking, demanding to buy a half. She even asked me to sell her half and give her the rest for nothing! Good grief! I guess after spending two days in here, thinking about it, she probably only had money for half. The whole thing cost twelve cents. She must have only had six cents. Now that I look back on it, I shoulda given her the whole damn thing. But, I made the mistake of telling her I would talk to my boss, I called Tony my boss even though we're equal partners to make it sound like I had no choice in the matter, wouldn't let me sell one half a cantaloupe. Then, she insisted I go ask him! So, I went inside to act like I was really gonna ask Tony. He was plucking chickens. I said to him 'Hey Tony, there's this ole hag bag out front wants to buy half a cantaloupe.' I see him looking past me like he seeing someone else. I turn around and it's her. So I said, 'and this lady wants to buy the other half.' That's when she swung a bag of what felt like rocks and hit me upside the head. Knocked me out. And she lost her balance, tried to stop her fall, and slipped on a tomato on the floor. Down she went, and me out cold, fell on top of her. Tony said she was screaming for me to get off her but I can't 'cause I'm dead to the world. Tony was trying to pull me off when the police showed up. And then, she told him I was trying to have my way with her! Good Lord, right in middle of the store? She landed on a bunch of turnip sacks, for crying out loud. And that's . . ."

"He said he'd be the second man killed that night," Stryker said slowly, pensively, consumed with his own thoughts.

"How's that?" Ray asked. He got no answer. "Whatcha say mister?"

"The police hadn't said a man was *murdered*. Montel shouldn't have known that." Stryker continued talking to himself, ignoring Raymond. "Doubt that big Sergeant remembers."

"Well, I ain't in here for murder," Ray said, sounding irritated. He lay back on the cot and wondered about how Tony was doing running the store alone.

The two men could only tell time by the meals they received. By counting the number of breakfasts they figured they'd been in jail four days. Conversation rarely passed between the two. Stryker never got around to acting friendly and Ray let the man be. The monotonous existence in total darkness was broken only by brief moments of light when meals were served. Finally, after the fifth breakfast, the cell door opened.

"Raymond, Mister Raymond B. Hamman!" The brightness flooding into the jail cell caused Ray and Stryker to put hands over their eyes, shielding them from the painful light. An eclipse of the jailor stood in the doorway. "Which one of you is Hamman?"

"I am." Ray raised a hand.

"Come with me."

Ray never came back to Stryker's cell. The old hag bag had offered to drop charges against Ray if Tony would sell her half a cantaloupe. He did, and she did. However, after several hours the cell door swung open again.

"In you go bub." The jailer gave a young man of slight build a push on the shoulder. "They let your old pal go, mister. Here's your new cell mate." The new inmate stumbled inside and the heavy door slammed shut. The sound of it reverberated in the hallway. The jailer imagined hearing the slamming of the door was particularly depressing for the prisoners and he liked that.

The new cell mate kept to himself at first. The only times Stryker knew he had company was when the new prisoner took meals and shit. It may have been the second day or the third one, Stryker had begun to lose count. He'd settled into existing in a void, a black void. The brick walls and the massive iron door blocked any outside noise from coming into the cell. Food trays appeared in the door slits where two times a day when he would pass his empty tray out in exchange for a fresh meal. Even if he made marks for days on the bricks, he couldn't see them, and why bother. How long he'd wait for a trial, presuming he got one, he couldn't guess, At least he'd be out of this hole for a while and he looked forward to it, regardless of the outcome. Once, while sleeping, he woke with hands caressing his chest and it took a moment to realize he wasn't dreaming. He ran his hands up the other man's torso to find his face. He slipped his left hand behind the man's head, and after locating his nose, he jammed the second and third fingers of the other hand, palm outward, up the nostrils as far as they would go. Then, he rolled violently toward the wall, dragging the fellow across his chest, and slammed his forehead into the brick. He rolled back and did that again. After the third time the man's body went limp and Stryker felt liquid running down the nose hand. Stryker withdrew his hands and shoved the man to the floor. He swung himself off his cot, lifted the unconscious cellmate by the back of his belt, and heaved him onto his own bunk. They had no more interaction after that.

Several days, or a week passed before the big iron door swung open again, Stryker couldn't tell. This time though, the jailer called his name. "Stryker, you're to come with me." Stryker covered his eyes with one hand and stumbled out of the cell. The guard took him by the arm and guided him down the corridor. Because of the sudden light, he was just as blind outside the cell as he was in it. They passed through two heavy gates and into another corridor which led to a set of stairs. If he squinted hard enough, he could barely see faint images under his hand as they descended the steps. At the bottom of the stairs, the guard guided him to a caged window where he retrieved the Peacemaker and gun belt, and an envelope from the overweight female guard.

"This is yours too," she said, handing him the sai. "What do you do with this thing?"

Stryker squinted heavily, still the icy steel stare behind his slitted eyes caused the woman to drop her gaze and look down at her desk. He took the three-pointed weapon and slid it into the pouch behind his back without answering.

"You need a bath." The woman scrunched up her nose. "Phew." She tried to counter his cold stare while shuffling papers.

Stryker felt the thickness of the envelope and figured its thickness close enough not to start a fight over missing dollars. He turned to leave, attempting to find the exit door with his limited vision. That's when the big sergeant from the hotel, stepped in front. The officer had obviously been waiting in the ground level office for Stryker's release. Stryker hadn't seen him waiting and cursed himself for the failing, even though his limited vision was not of his doing.

"Just because your lady friend found two old women to sign an affidavit saying you were in their room when they heard a gunshot don't mean you're in the clear bub. Stay in town here." Stryker raised his slitted eyes. They spewed deadly venom, and the sergeant was suddenly struck with the realization that here stood a man who could kill or be killed in a heartbeat, neither of which much mattered. The police uniform or what happened next would not spare the sergeant's life. He stood aside. "At least 'til we find the real murderer."

Stryker continued out the door, down another set of stairs to the street, and went to find a laundry and bath house. He ended up at Ah Toy's. There he bathed, with help of course. His clothes were wrapped in brown paper and sent out to be used as measurements for new ones. He opted out of the other services offered. Ah Toy brought him a robe to wear until his new clothes arrived. They drank tea and ate raw fish wrapped with seaweed in a private room adjacent to the larger reception area on first floor. Ah Toy wore the same style high-necked collar silk dress as before, long, and to the floor, with a side slit. Stryker remembered her prior dress, a red one. She wore black now. He thought her fingernails on her slender hands seemed longer, maybe because they were painted black.

"You meet you man?" She asked with a sculpted smile. The careless way in which she said the words, belied a more serious motive for the question.

"Yes, but not long enough. He left before we completed our business."

Ah Toy nodded politely.

Stryker studied the Asian's face. "Ah Toy, you know where he is."

"Yes, but . . . I not tell you."

Stryker waited, said nothing.

"You go see man, Bawee Blankton, he tell find Mista' Montel."

Stryker cocked an eyebrow. Ah Toy remembered who he was after. He wondered why she just didn't tell him herself of Montel's whereabouts. "Blankton will tell me? Why? He'll do it for you?"

"No, fo' you." Ah Toy bowed politely again.

"For me. You're sure." Stryker stated the question.

"Yes."

"Why?"

"Because you will hu't him bad. Then, he tell."

Stryker remained implacable, waiting. Nothing in his face gave away anything, however Ah Toy sensed he demanded more.

"He has how you say pawushuns."

"Perversions." Stryker offered.

Ah Toy dipped her head. "Yes, he hu't my girls. Some bad. One die. I tell him he no come again. Two months go by and taxes on Chinatown houses go way high. I hope he stubo'n man. Not tell quick where find Montel."

"Where do I find him?"

"At Sawo' Theate'. He not at Sawo' now. In two days you find him. He own theate'. I see you clothes come."

"He's not in San Francisco now." Stryker guessed.

Ah Toy blinked her long eyelashes.

Stryker rose to gather the new garments from the store courier. "You know many things, Ah Toy."

"House of Ah Toy have many . . ." She touched an ear with a long slender forefinger. Then she bowed and slipped out through a set of red silk curtains, behind which was another entrance Stryker had not seen. He shed the robe, laid it on the back of a chair, and put on the new trousers and shirt. As Stryker left Ah Toy's and started down the street toward the Palace, he pondered why he seemed to get along with prostitutes. Maybe, he thought, on the "hole" they were actually more honest than a lot of church folks. The corner of his mouth twitched.

Rather than heading straight to the hotel, he detoured to find and scout the Savoy. The building, more like a three story than just two, the front facing the street consisted of two levels, the back half raised up another level, making the rear of the Savoy three stories high. Stryker figured the third level accommodated the stage. Around back of the building, the ground fell away, since the theater stood on one of San Francisco's renowned hills. Running along the edges of the property, sides and rear, a wrought iron fence with spiked finial tips encouraged visitors to use the front entrance. He saw what he wanted and headed over to the Palace.

At the hotel, he discovered a room had been saved for him anytime he requested. That Hearst fellow was damn thoughtful, he thought. Too bad he hadn't gotten the document signed for him, the one the police confiscated and returned with no questions, unsigned by Montel. Failure, how he despised it. The clerk at the station must not have understood its importance, he guessed. He started to walk away from the hotel reception desk.

"Mister Stryker, you have a message."

Upon reading the note, he dropped it in the closest waste basket and took the rising room to the fifth floor. His long tan fingers held the key and turned it deliberately in the door lock, however, he pulled it out without reaching for the doorknob. He owed her thanks; hard for a man like him to do. But he walked back to the lift and told the operator "seventh floor."

Morgan opened the door after his knuckles rapped two times. She wore a navy blue satin robe, carelessly belted, loose and partially open at the breast, suggesting, or rather, inviting the soft curves be fully uncovered.

"Welcome back."

"I didn't get the damn thing signed yet." It came out as a protestation, and sounded like it. Here she was offering a reward, herself, as if he had been successful, come back victorious from a battlefield. No conquering hero here, Morgan.

"I know that," she said, sounding somewhat annoyed. A frown appeared, then quickly drained away.

The woman meant business.

But it's damn difficult for a man like Stryker to take something he hadn't earned. To be given that which he did not deserve went against his core, his values, against who he was. To be placed in this . . . situation, this awkward predicament . . . angered him. And when he felt a reaction stirring below his belt, betraying him, he became angrier. "God-dammit woman!"

Morgan certainly knew of the torments coursing through the man. In some regard, it gave her a sense of satisfaction, of pride, that she could affect the unaffectable. Not control, she wouldn't want that anyway, but influence, yes, she would like to have an influence on him. He surely influenced her! "Can't we put all that aside for the moment?"

Stryker scowled at Morgan for what seemed interminable minutes. She waited. Finally, he grabbed her shoulders and violently spun her around. Still gripping the shoulders he marched her across the floor and shoved her upper body down on the bed. She tried not to scream but an involuntary yelp escaped as he gripped the back of her neck and pinned her face down on the bedspread. He held her there, spreading her feet on the floor with two demanding kicks of his boot while he undid his trousers. Then he jerked the satin robe over her hips and onto her back exposing two white, firm buttocks. Still forcing her face into the blanket, he positioned his penis near her vagina, dripped spit on the tip and shoved. Morgan felt his probing manhood and pulled forward, shying away from the rough entry. He released her neck, grabbed a fistful of long dark hair, and pulled her back on him. He rammed in for full penetration and she responded with a loud grunt. He pulled out and rammed again. After several repeats, he held it in deep inside, and Morgan wiggled her ass. He gripped her butt cheek and gave a hard squeeze. Releasing her hair and wrapping his hand around her neck again, he began long smooth strokes in and out. Working his hand around the smooth skin of her rear, he found the exposed clitoris. He used his middle finger, making small circles on it. After several minutes of that, Morgan started a low groan, almost a deep growl, coming from down in her belly. It worked its way up and exploded, riding a rush of air out her mouth. Her body went rigid. She convulsed. He let her rest a minute and then started the stroking again. He reached up and grabbed her right wrist, and pulled her hand down under her, between her legs. Pressing her fingers onto her clitoris, he moved her fingers around, forcing her to make the tight little circles on herself. Once she caught on, he released her hand and filled both his with the cheeks of her ass. He guided her to four more orgasms before he exploded with a grunt of his own. He then flipped her over and shoved her onto the bed. When he re-entered, his eyes bored into hers, and he made her touch herself while he watched her come.

Later, they lay together, Morgan resting her head on him.

"You have trouble finding the two old women?" Stryker stared at the ceiling.

"Yes, but I found them." Morgan waited for the "thanks" she would not hear. Finally, she said, "You're welcome," as her fingers lightly caressed his chest.

Eventually, Stryker made it to his own room. From his window, he could see parts of the bay. He stood for a moment, looking out at the ships. He thought about paying Hearst a visit. Not yet though, only when he could hand over a signed deed. Waiting another day and half for Blankton seemed risky. Montel would surely learn he had gotten out of jail and the Frenchie might slip deeper into hiding. But even if he'd tried physical *persuasion* on Ah Toy, she wouldn't tell him about Montel. Tough lady, he could beat her unconscious and get nothing. Then, he would lose a friend. She sure wanted Blankton to get the shit kicked out of him.

Stryker decided to stay in the hotel room until night fall. When he went out, he walked to Chinatown for a meal. The strong smells took a while to get over, but growing up around it helped. He stopped and entered a soup house, small even by Asian standards. There were three tiny tables. He chose one next to a side wall where he could keep an eye on the door. He ate a bowl of noodles with cubes of duck stir-fried in it, and drank a cup of rice wine. Wearing the Peacemaker strapped to his right side drew no stares, but he did receive quick and courteous service. A light drizzle met him outside and he pulled his collar up under the Stetson during the walk back to the Palace.

What the hell was he going to do about Morgan?

He felt as if he was being drawn and quartered. Pulled by a damn fine woman, pulled by a new trail between the roan's ears that begged to be ridden, by the open night sky of a billion stars he could see lying on a bedroll, and pulled by . . . the Call of the West.

But a woman like Morgan only comes once in a life time, if at all. "Fuck." It was the only remark he could muster.

He stopped at the front desk. No new note. Good, he wanted to be left alone. However, when he stepped off the lift, strode to his door and opened it, he saw he had a visitor.

145

"Cossette." Stryker shed his coat and threw it across an empty chair by the one where she sat. His hotel room, less than half the size of Hearst's and also smaller than Morgan's, had a four poster seven-foot bed against one wall, a three-by-five foot mahogany desk with a straight back chair opposite the bed, a chest at the end of the bed, and a small round table with lamp in the corner. He unbuckled his gun belt and hung it on the bed post closest to the door. Cossette sat on the chair.

"Stryker." Cossette got to her feet. Receiving no response, she added, "I persuaded the maid to let me in." She turned behind her and picked up the violin, but she didn't sit. "I said I would play for you." She had on a simple knee-length dress, light blue, with lace adorning the collar and sleeves. It appeared clean, but it wasn't new. The blue looked washed out and the lace had melted from white to a light yellow. Even though faded, her blue dress still contrasted nicely with the cream colored wall paper. Her hair appeared freshly washed but not brushed and her face had the sallow pallor of a person who had suffered great stress. She sat and brought the violin to her chin. It seemed as if it took a supreme effort for her to begin to play because it was several minutes before the bow touched the strings.

Stryker, seeing a labored delay, sat on the bed, pulled off his boots, and lay back on the pillows. He folded his arms across his chest and crossed his feet.

Finally, Cossette began to play. The song she chose was *Nocturne.* He'd heard the haunting melody many years ago and liked it. It evoked sadness then, but that was gleeful compared to the way Cossette's violin wept tonight. She played with eyes closed, her body barely swaying, mournfully with the music. After a few moments, she paused. "Was he alive when you found him?"

"Yes."

"How was he?"

"Not good."

"There was a fire."

"He died before it started."

Cossette placed the bow on the violin and began again, picking up where she had left off with *Nocturne.*

Stryker watched her play. He wondered if the woman was experiencing grief up close for the first time. Consolation simply did not occur to him. He had always grieved alone. That is, until he got numb to it. All he knew to do now was lie there and watch tears crawl down her face.

Eventually, Cossette drew the bow across the strings for the last note and she stood, placing the violin on the desk. She turned toward him. A corner of her mouth rose in a futile attempt at a smile. "Thank you," she said, and she walked to the door. She opened it with care and closed it softly behind her.

Stryker closed his eyes and waited for Cossette's return.

A knock on the door woke him, seven hours later. He swung his feet to the floor, bent down and pulled on his boots. He glanced at the violin still resting on the desk and quickly stepped to the door and flung it open.

"Good morning Stryker." Morgan brushed by him and entered the room. "Did I surprise you?" She asked, sensing she had. She spied the violin. "I never knew you played."

"Cossette was here." Stryker got in front of it. "She asked about her husband. What time is it?" He asked, noticing it remained dark outside the window.

"About half past six. She was the French woman pretending to be Montel," Morgan said, proving she remembered Stryker's brief description of the Utah trip. She lightly ran her fingers along the bow strings. Morgan kept a dozen other questions stuffed down her throat and asked instead, "Did she play well?"

"Yes, and . . ." Stryker started to add she played sadly but he didn't. "Yes, she played well. She left last night and didn't take it, referring to the violin." He eyed the instrument as he spoke, trying to figure out what might have happened to Cossette.

"She say anything before she left?" Morgan asked.

"She thanked me. Why?"

"She jumped off the roof last night."

Morgan waited for a reaction. When none appeared she said, "George asked me about your progress yesterday. I came by earlier last night but you weren't here." She raised an eyebrow, as if to ask, were you really here? Again the mixed-breed remained impassive. "How about breakfast? You can tell me what to tell him. Half hour?" Not waiting for an acknowledgement, Morgan flipped around and headed out the door.

Stryker turned back to the desk. The violin, he thought, lay there as if left behind by mistake. He walked over and picked up the instrument. Up close he could see it was a good one, old and well used. He briefly held it in open palms then stepped over to open the window, and tossed it into the fog.

He used the wash bowl on a free-standing pedestal by the desk. Looking in the mirror, he ran the razor down his throat and scrapped off facial hair, leaving the shadow of a beard along the jaw line. He slicked back the long hair, which needed a cut, with more water, and splashed a little lilac water on his cheeks.

Lifting the gun belt from the bed post, he buckled it around his waist and picked the sai off the bed. He shoved it down between the belt and the small of his back. He left the room and went down the hall. When he got off the rising room lift at ground level, he walked out the portal to Market Street and a light rain. From there he turned north to the corner of Sutter, found a coffee shop with a folding sign displaying the breakfast menu on it and went inside. He'd eaten the fried eggs and sausage and had drunk half of the second cup of black coffee when Morgan found him.

"I guess I went to the wrong restaurant." She took a chair opposite Stryker at the table. "Fortunately, I saw you walk through the portal and realized you weren't coming to meet me. Just so you know, and in case you need reminding, you can be a real asshole."

"When I get the damn thing signed, he'll know it."

For whatever reason, Morgan didn't know why, Stryker's features hardened, his steel gray eyes narrowed to slitted glints of silver. "How's the coffee?" She asked, waving at the young man behind the counter, and then holding an invisible cup to her mouth.

"It'll do."

"Good. I also wanted to tell you, I'll be heading down the coast for a few days, looking at property for George." She returned fire with the usage of the Senator's first name.

Stryker didn't bother to analyze himself, why he was in such a shitty mood. He stayed irascible most of the time anyway and failed to notice he had different levels of it. He slapped a couple of dollars on the table and got to his feet. 'See you around Morgan."

Morgan didn't look to see which way Stryker turned when he went out the door. She drank the coffee as the young waiter picked up the dishes from Stryker's side of the table.

"Breakfast ma'am?" He asked.

She shook her head no.

Stryker figured the Blanktons wouldn't have arrived back in San Francisco as yet. However, he headed over to the Savoy anyway. The fog still hung heavy, so thick he had trouble finding street signs, but he still made it to the theater before eight. Maybe he should have skipped breakfast and arrived earlier, but the place looked deserted anyway, and that's how he wanted to find it. The main entrance doors, thick wooden behemoths, reinforced with broad metal straps and another single door, regular size, were locked. He went around to the side and then to the rear. In the back he found a door not as formidable and pried it open with the sai. The basement was one large storage area for props and equipment with small aisles for stages hands to use. Windows above the door Stryker came through allowed enough diffused light to cast the bigger fixtures and boxes as shadowed obstacles to avoid. He came to a stage lift where he figured it was positioned below center stage, but he chose not to attempt using it, and instead kept going until he found stairs. They took him to a very dark second level. The way his boots echoed on the wooden floor told him he had found the stage and cadaverous seating hall. Feeling his way along a wall he came to the front of the theater which had more light and he found another set of stairs. They took him up to the offices. He entered the one which had "Manager" on it.

Inside, a glass door with curtains on the opposite wall allowed some light in the room which had a large desk with chairs in front, a wing back leather chair behind, and a sofa on his right, all on plush dark red carpet. He brushed back the curtains and opened the glass door for additional lighting. Then he walked over to the sofa, plopped down facing the entry door, brought up his legs on the cushions, and crossed them. There he waited.

CHAPTER FIFTEEN

Barry and Phyllis Blankton were awakened Sunday morning by a porter with a tray of eggs, bacon, toast, juice, and coffee. Forty miles south of San Francisco, breakfast was being served to the Southern Pacific first class passengers prior to pulling into the city. Joined by eight other members of the Socialist Labor Party, the Blanktons had ventured south to Los Angeles in an effort to recruit and organize a southern faction of Marxist ideologues. Railroad strikes had galvanized the laborers to be more receptive to the Socialist movement springing up throughout the United States. Anarchists stoked the fires of dissent causing riots and the destruction of property. Holding boisterous gatherings, they planted associates among the crowd to arouse them. In addition, the Socialists published their own weekly newspaper, the *San Francisco Truth*, boldly named opposite of what it really stood for.

"I think we did well down south, Phil." Blankton called his wife Phil for short. "Brilliant idea of yours, bringing some of our men, putting them in the audience to act as unhappy locals. You're not just a pretty face."

"Save it, Barry," Phyllis retorted. He hadn't fucked her in twenty years. She'd easily put on sixty pounds since their marriage, and her puffy jowls drooped low enough to jiggle when she spoke. Her ass cheeks had sagged over a chair's edges for the past seven years. Both were in it for the politics. Romance existed outside the marriage. So what, it worked, except when Barry's excesses became too much. "I've been thinking. We may be going about this the wrong way."

Barry turned his head toward his wife, canting it to the side, the way a person does when wanting to appear puzzled. "How's that?"

"We've been trying to protect Alain from losing the *Examiner* to Hearst." Phyllis spoke slowly.

"Yeah?"

"While we had the fake Montel running all over the country to get that killer away from here, we missed a God-given opportunity." She nodded pensively, as if arriving at a profound truth, then fell silent.

"All right, Phyllis. Out with it." Blankton hated it when she acted mentally superior. But in fact, she was, and she possessed a ruthlessly cunning mind.

"If you didn't have a penis doing so much of your thinking, you might figure it out. We should have killed Hearst."

Blankton stared at his wife partially in disbelief and partially in admiration. "Is it too late?"

"Maybe . . . not. Eat your eggs."

The train pulled into San Francisco's Third and Townsend depot at ten past eight. From there the Blanktons took a horse-drawn cab to the Savoy Theater. Rain came down harder as they ran to a smaller front door beside the main entrance, and waited inside for their bags. Barry lit a lamp and had the cab driver carry their luggage upstairs to set it by a door labeled "Private." He tipped the man a nickel.

"Set them inside for now, Barry," Phyllis instructed. "We have work to do."

Barry unlocked their residence door and placed the bags inside, and then followed Mrs. Blankton down the hall to the office. That door was always left unlocked. Blankton opened it and stepped aside for his wife.

"Shit, you left the fucking balcony door open." The woman could leave a sailor awestruck.

"I'll close it," Blankton said. "I thought sure, I shut the damn thing." He was no match for her tongue. He brushed by his wife and swept past the desk to close the door.

'Leave it!" Stryker ordered. He'd gotten up from the couch. He fisted the sai from behind, flipped it in his hand, and poked Mrs. Blankton's back with the center tine. "Over by the desk." Stryker straightened the arm holding the sai, digging it into her back.

"Ow!" Mrs. Blankton jumped forward with a sudden start. She moved hurriedly to stand by her husband, behind the desk.

"Light the lamp." Stryker pointed the sai.

"I need matches." Blankton pulled the drawer open and reached inside.

Stryker flipped the sai backward in his hand, the three sharp tips pointing toward the floor. Leaping forward, he stabbed the weapon downward. The longest tine speared Blankton's hand, inches from the .32 caliber pistol.

"Aahhh!" Blankton tried to pull out his hand, but it was impaled to the bottom of the drawer.

"Where's Montel?" Stryker made small circular motions with the sai's handle, expanding the hole in the back Blankton's hand.

"Aahhh! God!" Blankton cried out in pain.

"God said you fucked up. Sent me."

Even without the lamp light, the Blanktons could see the facial features of the man some called evil. His ghostly eyes stared intensely into Blankton's, looking deadly, no sign of emotion.

"It's him!" Phyllis screamed. "Don't tell him, Barry!"

Stryker jerked the sai out of Blankton's hand, spun it again, and jabbed the bloody tine under the man's chin.

Blankton probably realized his wife just ascertained Blankton knew Montel's whereabouts, and now Stryker intended to get it out of him. "Run Phil!" Doubtful the warning to his wife was meant to save her. Instead, he more likely intended to rat out Montel and wanted to get the woman out of the room.

Stryker cupped the back of Blankton's neck with his free hand and shoved downward. The sai dug deeper.

"The *Marcy*!" Blankton scrunched his face, squeezing his eyes tightly together. "Please." He opened his eyes, pleading with them.

"Hotel," Stryker said, between gritted teeth. He pushed harder.

"Ship! It's a ship! Fisherman's . . ."

Stryker released Blankton's neck and lowered the point of the sai a couple inches.

"You bastard!" Phyllis screamed at her husband. For a woman of her age and girth, she moved with surprising agility, striking Blankton's shoulders with outstretched arms, shoving him off balance. Blankton, caught off guard by his wife's attack, stumbled backward, tripping over his own feet. He attempted to right himself by clutching at the door jam, but that effort only served to keep him upright until he continued across the three foot balcony and flipped over the railing. Strangely, Blankton remained silent as he fell. He landed face down and lengthwise on the spiked fence below. The sharp finial tips riveted his torso to the fence from his open mouth to his groin. Although his distributed weight kept the spikes from puncturing completely through his body, enough found vital organs to kill him. But not instantly. Mrs. Blankton watched in horror from the balcony above as his body wiggled and struggled . . . until the butt of Stryker's Peacemaker struck the back of her skull.

Fifteen minutes later she woke to find herself sitting, more accurately, slumping, on a straight back chair downstairs in the middle of the stage floor, with a rope around her neck. The rope tightened, pulling her body upright. She tried to scream for help but the rope kept getting tighter, pulling higher. She somehow managed to get to her feet, and step up on the chair.

Stryker came round in front of her. Mrs. Blankton, consumed with fear, stared down at him, eyes opened wide. "What are you . . .?" She rose up on her toes. "Why? You . . . got . . . aahh!" She nearly lost her balance.

Stryker put his boot on the front of the chair and shoved. He left the Savoy the same way he came in and started off for Fisherman's Wharf. "Payback is hell," he growled outloud.

Monday's *Examiner* ran the morning headline–"TRAGEDY AT SAVOY." The text of the news article recounted how Barry Blankton tragically fell from the third floor balcony of the theater, impaling himself on the spiked fence surrounding the property. Mrs. Blankton, evidently overcome with grief upon seeing her husband's gruesome death, decided to take her own life. Her body was found hanging by a rope Sunday afternoon. The cleaning crew found her when they came to work at two o'clock. The same column continued with brief biographies of both, espousing their many acts of self-sacrifice and charity. Most of the readers who saw the piece, accepted the author's writing extolling the Blankton's virtues at face value. However, there was one who did not. Upon reading the article, a wry, pleasant smile, crept onto the painted white face of a certain Asian madam in Chinatown.

Stryker walked out onto the street from the Savoy, and although rain came down so that only the hearty braved it, he decided to walk part of the way to Fisherman's, choosing not to catch a cab in front of the Savoy. He bent into the hill and rain but half way up Leavenworth to Nob Hill and he flagged down a cab. The driving rain came inside the buggy anyway. Fifteen minutes later, the driver pulled to a stop at the ocean steamer, *Marcy*, moored at the west end of the wharf. Being Sunday and with the rain coming down in a torrential downpour, all hands were either below deck or not aboard. Stryker saw no one on deck when he stepped off the gangplank. Although it was mid-morning, the wretched weather blocked the sun and it felt as if it could be anywhere half-way between dusk and midnight. Stryker kept one hand on the railing and one over his brow under the hat brim, searching for a door to the decks below. He found one mid-ship, located under a set of stairs. There, he ran into a ship's mate. The fellow was struggling to cover a pallet of newly delivered cabinet doors. The pounding rain kept Stryker from hearing the cursing until he came up behind the man.

"Looking for a Frenchman," Stryker shouted above the storm.

The mate, too busy tying down the tarp to turn around, yelled back, "Bottom deck, last cabin at the bow!"

Stryker angled behind the man and reached for the door's levered handle. He stepped through the watertight doorway. The first thing he noticed inside the passageway was that he'd escaped the damn rain. He spied another airtight doorway to his right and opened it to a stair ladder heading below. He climbed down it and then three more until he came to a floor with no more ladders going lower. The dim passageway was lit by two flickering lights, each about one-third from the ends of the hallway. The steam engine pistons, although running idly, knocked loudly in the engine room, reverberated off the metal walls. The heavy smell of oil permeated the air. Heat from the engine room brought the temperature in the passageway to a stuffy eighty-something degrees and Stryker wondered what the hell Montel was doing in such a pathetic hideout. A sense of satisfaction swept through him when he figured the Frenchie suffered these uncomfortable accommodations just to hide from him. The right corner of his lip twitched.

The last two doors on left side of the corridor were marked "Maintenance." He tried the end one on his right. Unlocked, or the lock broken, the door swung easily open. A light quick step through the doorway, and he moved inside, closing the door behind him.

Stryker drew and cocked the Peacemaker in one swift fluid motion. Montel leapt from the bed and reached for his coat. He froze with his hand barely a foot away from the derringer in the pocket.

"Throw the coat on the floor and pick up the pen." Stryker pointed with the Colt at the pen and ink bottle resting on a small writing desk. With his free hand, he pulled a leather pouch and threw it on the table. "Open it and sign."

Montel slipped the jacket off the chair, letting it fall to the floor, and picked up the pouch. He held it in two hands without opening it. "I sign this and you leave. I stay alive?" He asked, pleading with raised eyebrows.

"Sign it."

Montel hesitated, then he untied the packet, and withdrew the four papers. He unfolded them and dipped the pen in the ink. After carefully signing along the designated lines on each page, he re-folded the document.

Stryker held out his free hand and Montel handed the papers to him. Stryker kept the Colt aimed at Montel as he sifted through the pages, inspecting the signings. "Put them back in." He gave the papers back to Montel.

The Frenchman stuffed them back into the leather pouch. He reached out his arm to hand the packet to Stryker, drew it back to his lap, and re-tied the rawhide strings. "Here, mister." He stood and held out the hand holding the pouch. "That's all you . . . ?"

Without warning the door burst open, banging into Stryker's back, shoving him past Montel.

"Get your lazy ass topside, Pierre!" The ship's boss stevedore, a squat burly ball of hard muscles and tenacity, threw the gruff order through the open door.

Montel broke for the door. Stryker grabbed for the pouch. It came hurtling out of the Frenchman's hand, landing by his coat lying on the floor. Montel dashed out of the cabin, brushing past the startled loading foreman.

Stryker holstered the Colt, sprang across the cabin, and picked up the pouch. He stuffed it in his coat pocket.

The stevedore glanced at Montel running down the passageway and turned back to Stryker coming through the door.

"Who the fuck are you?" He shoved with both hands to push the mixed-breed back in the cabin.

Stryker cupped both hands and chopped down on the knotty forearms, pulling the stout man toward him. In an upward rolling movement he swung both fists up to punch the puffy face. Stepping into the man, Stryker hooked his left arm behind the man's round head and smashed his right elbow into the man's temple. The stunned man sagged back against the wall and before he could gather his senses, Stryker sprinted down the passageway.

Stryker reached the stair ladder, ruefully thinking riding boots are made for riding not running.

Montel ran at full stride once he hit the wharf. He ran nearly four hundred yards in the driving rain. With his chest burning and legs wobbly he was forced to stop. Bent over, breathing heavily, hands on knees, he canted his head left and saw the last of the passengers boarding the Sausalito ferry.

A couple minutes later, the ferry pulled away from the dock. The Frenchman stood alone at the bow. Everyone else stayed below deck out of the rain. Montel had to run now and he wanted no one to see him, recognize him. He was still trying to catch his breath and figure out how Stryker tracked him down. As far as he knew only the

Blanktons knew where he hid out and he'd used a fake name on the ship. Why would the Blanktons, if they had, betray him? The rain drove in from the front and he turned toward the stern.

A shadow? Did he see the shadow of another man? Montel asked himself. He hurriedly wiped the rain from his eyes and looked again. Yes, he realized, there's a man, walking toward him along the rail.

It's him! He's on the ferry! Montel screamed in his head. He's got the deed. What does he want now? Only one thing, one reason, he thought, terrified at the obvious conclusion. He's on this boat, walking toward Montel because he's coming to kill him.

As Stryker came on, he remained motionless, rooted in place and watched, as if an animal in shock, waiting for the death blow. Stryker walked slowly, carefully. He stopped directly in front of Montel. And the Frenchman merely stood there, arms hanging by his sides.

Suddenly, Stryker's arm flashed out, his hand grazed Montel's throat. Montel felt a slight tug, thinking Stryker merely meant to scare him. Why? He thought. Just shoot me!

Montel sensed a stinging in his throat. His legs grew weak. Then he saw Stryker wipe the razor on a sleeve. Montel coughed and felt the rattle in his windpipe. He started to slump. He turned to grip the railing. The rain pelted his face and his head bowed forward, over the railing. An arm cradled his legs at the knees, then lifted his legs up and flipped him over the top rail. Down he went into the black water. Salt water stung the cut and foam from the wave splashed in his eyes When he bobbed to the surface, the ship's bow brushed by, the steel hulk scraped repeatedly against his body until the ferry passed. The wake swamped him and he fought to keep his head above the waves. For a brief moment he thought of swimming to the distant lights on shore. He stretched out his arms to dog paddle but his hands slowly sank to his sides, and he rolled forward sliding beneath the waves.

Hearst, in his room at the Palace, heard two solid raps. He rose from the desk chair by the window and went to open the door.

"Hello, Stryker." Hearst turned and crossed the floor to the table, an invitation for Stryker to follow. Hearst drew out a cigar from the drawer, lit it, puffed three hearty draws, and poured two fingers of Scotch into a glass. He turned to Stryker. "How about you?"

"No thanks." Stryker pulled the pouch from his coat pocket and handed it to the Senator. "I signed too, as witness."

Hearst sat the glass on the table and took the pouch, holding the cigar in his hand. He unwound the string around the leather, reached inside and withdrew the documents. After sifting through the four pages, he looked up from them at Stryker, and nodded with a smile that suggested his gratitude. "I imagine Mister Montel wasn't all that happy to sign these. Do you think he'll give me more trouble?"

"No."

"Good, I'll make the deposit in the morning. And Stryker—you done me a great favor. I think William is gonna, well, you know he ain't done much 'cept travel around Europe with his mother. I think he's gonna do something with the *Examiner*, make himself a life with it. I have a feeling the money and your effort will be worth it. By the way, you might like to know Morgan's in San Jose."

Stryker spun around to leave.

"Stryker, one more favor I must ask. If my son turns to shit after I'm gone, shoot him."

Stryker turned and tipped the Stetson. "So long, Senator."

Stryker walked out of the Palace and caught the cable car to the Ferry House. The roan was delivered while he drank coffee and waited. He threw all the personal possessions he had, stuffed in the one carry bag, behind the saddle. Stryker tied it down and climbed up on the horse. He headed south.

A day and a half later Stryker came to a road sign. The sign read "San Jose Twelve Miles" with an arrow pointing straight ahead, "Pescadero Eighteen Miles" with an arrow pointing right. He reined in the roan. After sitting in the saddle for several minutes, Stryker pressed his boots into the roan's flanks and flapped the reins, starting down the road to Pescadero.

A month later, Stryker, still in Pescadero, lay on his bare chest, receiving a daily massage from a mixed-breed woman named, Elena. A woman of thirty and a widow of four years ran a boarding house in the small town, approximately one mile from the Pacific coast. During the month, she had taken a liking to the tall stranger who'd ridden into town on a big roan horse, but he remained a mystery and she knew practically nothing about him. Every morning, he would ride out to the sea, return, and relax in the afternoons. He drank sparingly, talked even less. After ten days she offered back rubs as part of her hospitality. She'd told him she did it for all her guests. However, that was a lie and he knew it. It was one of those lies which are told where the liar and the "liee" both know and acknowledge it with unspoken good-natured acceptance. At first, he kept on his shirt, but lately she had requested he remove it so she could apply oil to sooth the muscles.

"Mister Stryker, these scars you have on your back, are they all from the 'wimen' you make love?" She asked, as she ran a finger down the length of one.

"Not all," he grunted.

Elen smiled to herself. "I am almost finished. I'll go get your cold beer and be back. She walked out of his room and down two floors to her basement where she kept milk, butter, and of course, bottled beer for her guests, the one guest, really.

Stryker sat up and reached for his shirt. He'd been reading the *Examiner* prior to the massage and it lay open on the desk in his room. A small notice in the classified section caught his attention. Outlined with a heavy black rectangular line, it read . . .

"To N.S. Another job is requested by G.H. He would like to hear from you at your earliest convenience, and so would I. M.B."

Elena returned with the beer. She watched as Stryker tucked in his shirt and strapped on his gun belt. "You going somewhere Mister Stryker?"

"San Francisco."

ABOUT THE AUTHOR

Wes Rand grew up in Tennessee. After serving in the United States Army as an artillery officer, he moved to the West. He plans to live the rest of his life under the open skies of Nevada and Utah.

"PAYBACK IS HELL" is Rand's third book in the Evil Stryker Series. It is a follow on to his first two successful novels, "LEFT TO DIE" and "CROSS CUT." His next book in the series, "IT WAS TO DIE FOR" will be available next year.

Thanks to Ray Seakan, Colonel Robert Tone, and special thanks to my editor, Lee Barnes.